# WHERE THE BOYS ARE

# WHERE THE BOYS ARE

## JOHN HALL

SCHOLASTIC INC.
New York Toronto London Auckland Sydney

No part of this publication may be reproduced in whole or in part, or stored in a retrieval system, or transmitted in any form or by any means, electronic, mechanical, photocopying, recording, or otherwise, without written permission of the publisher. For information regarding permission, write to Scholastic Inc., Attention: Permissions Department, 555 Broadway, New York, NY 10012.

ISBN 0-590-05960-2

12 11 10 9 8 7 6 5 4 3 2 1        8 9/9 0 1 2 3/0

Printed in the U.S.A.        01

First Scholastic printing, August 1998

Thanks again to my editor, Ann Reit, who asked for Ben's story and gave me the chance to tell it.

To Amy Griffin, who works behind the scenes making my books better.

And to Marie Sproull, my good friend in Virginia.

To my father, who's taught
me so much.
This one's for you, Dad.

# Chapter 1

"The bottom of your ice cream cone is dripping."

Seventeen-year-old Ben Harris looked down at his ice cream cone and groaned. There were already three drops of triple chocolate fudge splattered across the front of his new white shorts. As another drop of chocolate began to fall, he stuck the pointed tip of his cone into his mouth.

"I hate eating an ice cream cone this way," he complained to his best friend, Ray Preston.

"You should have ordered a wafer cone. They never drip," Ray said, licking his double swirl of vanilla and chocolate covered with colored sprinkles. "So what do you want to do now?" he asked as they left the ice cream shop and headed out into the mall. "We've got twenty minutes to kill before the movie starts."

"Keep your eyes open for any help-wanted signs," Ben urged.

"Still no luck finding a summer job?"

Ben shook his head. "I've filled out applications all over town. You name it, I've been there. Pizza parlors. Supermarkets. Video stores. Auto garages. I haven't gotten one phone call yet."

"You know, you're not the only one searching for a summer job," Ray said.

"Hey, look!" Ben exclaimed. He pointed to a help-wanted sign in the window of a bookstore. "I'll be right back!"

Five minutes later, after talking with the store manager, Ben was dragging his way out of the bookstore.

"What happened?" Ray asked, rolling up the sports magazine he was reading and sticking it in the back pocket of his shorts.

"The job's already filled," Ben said. "They hired someone yesterday afternoon." He sighed and dabbed at the chocolate stains on the front of his shorts. "I guess this isn't my day."

Ray slung an arm around Ben's shoulders. "Cheer up, Ben! It's the first week of summer vacation. We've got two months of uninterrupted fun ahead of us. No classes. Sleeping in. Late-night partying. Swimming and surfing."

"Easy for you to say," said Ben. "You have a job." Ray was working at Dog Gone Clean, a dog grooming shop where customers could bring in their dogs and rent tubs to wash them. Or have someone like Ray do the washing. "I don't."

"Don't worry. You'll find something."

"Where?" Ben asked.

"Berkley Heights isn't the only town hiring for the summer," Ray pointed out. "Have you thought about looking for a job in Southvale?"

"I never even thought of Southvale," Ben stated. Southvale was a nearby town, an hour away, and very popular during the summer. Many families vacationed in Southvale because it was located right next to a beach.

"Do you think I'd have any luck?" Ben asked.

Ray nodded, his dark brown curls bouncing up and down. "My parents and I were there over the weekend. We had lunch at the new country club and hotel that opened. The Southvale Swim and Sun Club. It overlooks the beach and it's really classy. I'll bet they're hiring for the summer. Let's grab a newspaper and check it out."

Ben tried not to get too excited, but a summer job at the Southvale Swim and Sun Club could help him start building up his college fund. It wasn't like he really *needed* a summer job. He had spending money because his parents gave him a weekly allowance. They preferred that he concentrate on keeping up his grades and didn't want him to work during the school year. But his weekly allowance wasn't going to be enough when it came time for college next year.

Ben knew his parents would do their best to pay for his college education, but there were always bills and expenses that had to be paid first. He hoped that, because his grades were solid, he might win a full or partial scholarship, but he couldn't count on that. And he didn't think it was fair to expect his parents to pay for four years of college. He wanted to contribute as much as he could.

Ray stopped at a newsstand and plunked down fifty cents. "You can pay me back after you get your first paycheck."

"Big spender," Ben said, snatching up a newspaper. "Does this mean you're paying for the movie tickets, too?"

Ray cupped his ear. "What'd you say, Ben? Speak up. I'm having a little trouble hearing you."

Ben gave Ray a playful shove. "Yeah, right," he answered, scanning through the newspaper. He stopped when he reached the help-wanted ads and let out a shout of glee. "You were right! Take a look at this!"

Ray followed Ben's finger to the ad he was pointing to.

"Southvale Swim and Sun Club," Ray read aloud. "Looking for waiters, busboys, valets, golf caddies, and desk clerks. Interviewing from eight to twelve on Tuesday, June twenty-eighth."

"That's tomorrow," Ben said.

"I guess I know where you're going to be tomorrow morning at eight o'clock," Ray said.

Ben nodded his head. "Absolutely. The early bird catches the worm and tomorrow I plan on catching a job!"

"Ben, wake up. Wake up!"

"Go away," Ben mumbled, burying himself deeper under the sheets at the sound of his mother's voice. She started shaking his shoulder. "Leave me alone."

His eleven-year-old brother, Dougie,

poked him in the side. "Are you training for the Sleep Olympics?"

With his eyes still closed, Ben reached out from under the sheets and swatted at his brother. "Beat it, shrimp."

"Ben," his mother repeated, "are you getting up? I thought you had a job interview this morning."

Ben lifted his head up off his pillow and opened his eyes. He yawned and pushed his blond bangs off his forehead. "I do."

"Well, don't you think you'd better get moving?" She walked over to the window and pulled up the shades. Bright bursts of sunlight streamed into the dark room, making Ben squint. "The morning's almost over."

"Almost over?" A feeling of dread spread through Ben's stomach. "What time is it?"

"Ten o'clock," Dougie answered.

Ben jumped out of bed. "Ten o'clock!" he exclaimed. "Why'd you let me sleep so late? I wanted to be at Southvale by eight o'clock so I could be one of the first in line for an interview."

Ben's mother turned from the window, arms folded across her chest. "Don't blame me, young man. I've been calling you for the last hour. You didn't tell me what time you had to be out of the house. All you said was you had an interview in the morning."

"Yeah," Dougie piped in. "Don't blame Mom. Who told you to stay up late watching the *Twilight Zone* marathon on the Sci-Fi Channel?"

"You're just mad because Mom wouldn't let you stay up with me and Ray to watch it," Ben said, searching through his closet for a pair of khakis.

"I'm heading downstairs. Do you want any breakfast?" Mrs. Harris asked.

"Thanks, but I don't have any time," Ben answered, finding the khakis he wanted, along with a white shirt.

Ben raced into the bathroom and quickly ran a toothbrush through his mouth. He struggled with his hair, trying to get it to stay down instead of sticking up in all directions. He finally gave up, slicked it back with gel, and then quickly dressed.

"Did you tape it for me?" Dougie asked when Ben returned to his bedroom.

"Tape what?" Ben asked, searching for his penny loafers. Where were they? He hadn't worn them since the last day of school, a week ago, and he didn't see them anywhere. His bedroom was a mess, with CDs, books, magazines, and clothes scattered across the floor.

Dougie huffed. "The *Twilight Zone* marathon."

Ben shoved his brother to one side as he searched under a pile of shorts and T-shirts. "Maybe I did and maybe I didn't."

"Ben . . ." Dougie whined. "You promised!"

Ben found his scuffed penny loafers under his bed and jammed his feet into them. Snatching a green striped tie off his dresser, he pulled it over his head, tightening the knot. As he ran down the stairs to the front door, Ben called out to his brother, "Yes, I taped it for you. I even rewound the tape. It's all ready to go."

Dougie leaned over the banister. "Thanks, Ben! You're the best."

"Remember that the next time you decide to bug me," Ben said.

"Drive carefully," Mrs. Harris called from the kitchen.

"I will," Ben promised, hurrying out the front door.

In the driveway, he slid behind the wheel of his Dodge. It was at least ten years old and needed a new coat of paint, but the radio worked and it got him where he wanted to go.

After buckling up, Ben started the car and eased out onto the street.

As he was driving, Ben kept scolding himself for goofing up big-time. He'd heard his alarm go off at seven o'clock, but instead of getting out of bed the way he should have, he kept pressing the snooze button. Again. And again. And again.

Staying up until one o'clock in the morning hadn't helped, either. He should have gone to sleep early so he'd have had a good night's sleep. So he'd look refreshed instead of wrinkled. He'd wanted to iron his khakis and shirt. And he'd wanted to polish his penny loafers. Making a good impression counted for a lot.

Ben stopped at a red light and glanced at the time on his watch. Ten-fifteen. He hoped he wouldn't run into any traffic, but more important that there'd still be a job waiting for him when he arrived at the Southvale Swim and Sun Club.

Ben made it to the club with fifteen minutes to spare. He had run into some road construction on the drive over. As a result, it had taken Ben an extra thirty minutes.

Leaving his car in the parking lot, Ben hurried to the lobby.

"Excuse me," he asked a redheaded receptionist. She had green eyes and a small scattering of freckles across her nose. She seemed to be the same age as he was. "Could you tell me where the job interviews are being held?"

She gave Ben a warm smile and he noticed the small brass plate pinned on her white blouse. It had her name on it: Ashley.

"Second floor. In the dining room," she answered. "You better hurry. Gladys is almost finished."

"Gladys?"

"She's the one interviewing," Ashley explained.

"Thanks," Ben said.

"No problem," she replied.

As Ben hurried to the second floor, he couldn't help but notice his surroundings. The Southvale Swim and Sun Club reeked of money. Everything was so new and polished! The rugs covering the lobby floor were thick and plush. The furniture was gleaming. The windows sparkled and there were fresh flowers everywhere.

At the top of the stairs, Ben stopped in front of a mirrored wall and studied his reflection. He was a little bit nervous, so he took a deep breath to calm himself down. He always felt this way when he was meeting new people for the first time. He always wondered what they would think of him.

He straightened his tie and made sure his shirt was neatly tucked in. He looked okay. He wasn't the type of guy who usually turned heads, but he was nice-looking. Blond hair. Blue eyes. Nice straight teeth thanks to two years of braces in junior high. Six feet tall and slightly muscular from playing volleyball and basketball.

Satisfied with the way he looked, Ben turned away from his image and started searching for the dining room. He found it at the end of the hall. Inside, seated behind an ornate French desk, was a slender, gray-haired woman. Piled in front of her were a stack of applications.

"Is it too late to apply for a job?" Ben asked. He noticed that there was no one else around. Not a good sign. It could mean all the jobs were gone.

She lowered her glasses halfway down her nose and studied Ben. "It depends," she answered. "What kind of job are you looking for ?"

"Waiter?"

She shook her head. "All gone."

"Busboy?"

"Ditto," she replied.

"Valet?" Ben asked hopefully.

"I just hired my last valet. And receptionist. And desk clerk and golf caddy."

Ben fought the sinking feeling in his stomach. He'd messed up in a major way and he
didn't have anyone to blame but himself.

"Do you have *any* jobs left?" Ben asked,
trying to keep the disappointment out of his
voice.

The woman pushed her glasses back up
her nose and began flipping through a
folder. "Well, I do have something," she began, "but I don't know if you'd be interested
in it."

"I'll take it," Ben quickly said.

"But you don't even know what the job
is!" the woman exclaimed.

"As long as it pays, I'm interested," Ben
replied.

The woman began tapping on the front of
her folder with a pen. "What's your name?"
she asked.

"Ben. Ben Harris."

"I'm Gladys." She pointed to the chair in
front of her desk. "Take a seat."

Ben slid into the chair and accepted the
application Gladys handed to him. "Fill this
out and then we'll talk."

After Ben finished filling out the application, Gladys read the information he'd pro-

vided. "You live in Berkley Heights. That's quite a drive."

"I'll make sure I'm here on time," Ben promised.

Gladys raised an eyebrow. "Like today?"

Ben blushed. "I overslept. But it won't happen again."

Gladys laughed. "I like honesty. Well, Ben, like I said, I do have a job available. If you want it, it's yours.

"What's the job?" Ben asked.

"Maid."

"Maid?" Ben repeated.

Gladys nodded her head. "At the hotel, we call them chambermaids. You know, you make beds. Clean rooms. Vacuum. Wash windows and toilets. Replace dirty towels. That sort of thing."

"Isn't that a girl's job?" Ben asked. He could just imagine his friends laughing at him. They'd probably ask him where his feather duster was!

"It's a *job*," Gladys stated. "Anyone can do it. Anyone can do anything they set their mind to. Male or female." She stared at Ben over the rims of her glasses. "I thought you wanted a job."

"I do," Ben insisted. "I guess I didn't see myself cleaning rooms."

"You clean your room at home, don't you?"

"When my mom gets on my case to do it," Ben admitted.

"This is the same thing," Gladys stated. "Only you're cleaning ten rooms. Every day. Plus you'll make minimum wage and tips."

"Tips?"

Gladys smiled. "I thought that would get your attention. Yes, tips. Maids get tips. Most guests usually leave something at the end of the week to show their appreciation. So, what do you say, Ben? Do you want the job or not?"

Ben thought long and hard. He was desperate for a summer job. So far, nothing had come his way. What if he turned down this one and another summer job didn't come along?

Cleaning rooms couldn't be *that* bad. And he would be getting paid. With tips!

"Ben?" Gladys's voice broke into his thoughts. "Have you made up your mind or should I find someone else?"

"No," Ben quickly answered, afraid Gladys would withdraw her offer. "I'll take it!"

# Chapter 2

Ben inspected the room he had just finished cleaning, making sure everything was in order. The two beds were neatly made, with the bedspreads sharply creased and the pillows fluffed up. The furniture was dust free and the wastebasket in the corner was empty. In the bathroom, the faucets were shining, the mirror above the sink was sparkling, and clean towels were hanging from the towel rack.

Before locking the door behind him, Ben gave the room a quick spray of air freshener — mountain pine — and then headed for his cart out in the hallway.

As Ben pushed his cart in front of him, he thought of his job. Tomorrow would be the end of his first week as a maid. He had to admit, when he'd accepted the job he'd thought it would be easy. But it wasn't.

There was more to cleaning a room than just making the bed. Every day he vacuumed the rugs and drapes and scrubbed bathtubs and toilets. Sheets had to be changed and there were always wet towels to bring down to the hotel laundry room.

He had ten rooms to clean inside the hotel, in addition to five bungalows that lined the beach. He started cleaning at ten o'clock, since most guests were out of their rooms by then, and usually finished by three. Before entering any room with his master key, he always knocked first and called out, "Housecleaning."

So it wasn't the most fun summer job around. It was still a job. Ben knew he didn't have anything to complain about. He was making a weekly salary and yesterday he'd received his first tip from a couple checking out. There were also some unexpected perks. Employees were allowed to use the hotel pool and meals could be bought in the dining room at a discount.

So far, Ben hadn't used the hotel pool. Most afternoons, kids his own age were swimming in it. He wasn't usually the type to avoid making new friends, but he didn't want to be friends with these kids. He heard the nasty way they spoke to the waiters and waitresses who took their lunch and snack orders. He saw the way they bossed them around and played nasty jokes. Just because their parents were rich, they thought they were better than the hotel staff.

Ben didn't want to waste his time on jerks like that. Besides, they wouldn't want to be friends with him. Especially not if they knew he cleaned the rooms they slept in. Not that they knew he worked at the hotel. His cleaning uniform wasn't ready yet, so he worked in his own clothes. Ben couldn't understand how a person could be judged by a job and how much money he had, rather than the person he was on the inside.

Ben checked the time on his watch. Twelve-thirty. All he had left to clean were the bungalows and then he'd be finished for the day. Of course, he'd be finished much sooner if it wasn't for Bungalow E. No one was staying in it, but every day he had to clean it.

It didn't make sense to Ben. When he'd asked Gladys why the bungalow had to be cleaned *every day,* she told him that the family renting it for the summer didn't know when they'd be arriving, but they expected the bungalow to be spotless.

Fifteen minutes later Ben was inside the

bungalow, opening the windows. Because the bungalow wasn't being used, the air inside was stale and stuffy. Soon a cool summer breeze was wafting through the bungalow as Ben sprayed lemon-scented polish over the furniture.

Ben had just finished wiping down the top of a dresser when he heard a shout outside.

"Astrid! Astrid, come down!"

Ben stopped dusting and listened more closely. He heard a foot stomp. "Oooh! Sometimes you make me so mad! I should leave you up there. That would teach you a lesson!"

Curious to know what was going on outside, Ben abandoned his dusting. Standing in the open doorway, he looked around but didn't see anybody. He didn't hear anything. All was quiet. He was getting ready to head back inside when he heard the voice again. Louder. And much closer.

It was coming from next door. From Bungalow F.

Ben walked over to the white picket fence that divided the two bungalows. He stuck his head over the fence.

There was a girl on the other side. She had her back to Ben and was standing at the foot of a tree, staring up into the branches.

"Astrid!"

Ben wondered who Astrid was. Her little sister? A second later, he had his answer when a low-pitched yowl emerged from the leafy branches.

A cat. Her cat was stuck in the tree.

Ben studied the girl from behind. She had shoulder-length black hair worn in a pony-tail and tied with a white ribbon. She was wearing cutoff denim shorts, white sandals, and a red sleeveless blouse. Her arms and legs were nicely tanned. He hadn't seen her around before. She was probably a new guest at the hotel.

"Astrid, what am I going to do? I can't climb up there!"

Ben shook his head. Poor little rich girl. She probably expected someone to climb up the tree for her. Well, her cat could stay up there, for all he cared; he had to get back to work.

But then she turned around and Ben's mouth dropped open. He couldn't believe his eyes. She was gorgeous.

She ran over to the fence and reached for Ben's hand. The action caught him by sur-prise.

"Could you help me?" she asked anx-iously. Her green eyes were filled with worry. "My cat's stuck in the tree."

Ben couldn't find his tongue. She was the most beautiful girl he'd ever met. Her hand felt so smooth and soft. And he could smell the perfume she was wearing. It was light and flowery.

She gave Ben a puzzled look. "Do you understand English?" she asked, slowly spacing out her words. "Are you deaf?"

Ben found his tongue. "No, I'm not deaf and I understand English."

Relief washed over her face. "My cat's stuck in the tree," she repeated. "Could you get her down for me?"

"I'll try," Ben said. He walked around the fence and headed over to the tree.

Ben couldn't remember the last time he'd climbed a tree, but it all came back to him. As he drew closer to the top and the branch where Astrid was perched, Ben realized something. He gazed down at the bottom of the tree, where the girl was staring up at him.

"She's not going to scratch me, is she?" he asked.

The girl hesitated a second, but then answered quickly, "Of course not."

"Are you sure?" Ben asked suspiciously. "It took you awhile to answer."

"Well, she might," the girl admitted.

"That's why cats have claws. To defend themselves."

"But I'm not going to hurt her," Ben said. "I'm rescuing her."

"She doesn't know that," the girl stated in a tone that said Ben should know the same thing. "To her, you're a stranger. Astrid doesn't like strangers."

"Great," Ben muttered as he drew closer along the branch to Astrid. She was a black cat with gold eyes. And she didn't look pleased to see Ben. "Nice kitty. Nice Astrid."

Astrid hissed as Ben reached out for her. She struck out with a paw, claws bared.

"Don't hurt her," the girl called.

Ben stuck a scratched finger in his mouth. "What about her hurting *me*?" he called back.

Astrid began inching away from Ben, but Ben was determined not to let her get away. Taking a deep breath, he reached out for her, wrapping his hands around her middle.

"Gotcha!" Ben exclaimed.

Astrid didn't like being held and let Ben know it. She struggled in his grasp, trying to break free, making it hard for Ben to keep his balance.

"Don't drop her," the girl shouted. "Promise you won't drop her!"

That was the one thing Ben wanted to do.

Tightening his hold on Astrid, who was still scratching and hissing, Ben began inching back toward the tree trunk. Once he was there, he could let Astrid go and she would climb back down.

But then something happened.

Something Ben hadn't expected.

He heard a crack.

The tree branch was breaking.

Ben let go of Astrid, who jumped over to the tree trunk and raced down the tree. Ben tried to reach for the branch above him, but it was too late.

He was falling.

Falling . . .

# Chapter 3

Ben landed with a splash.

He'd fallen into the swimming pool under the tree.

Ben swam to the side of the pool. He expected to find the girl waiting to help him out, offering a hand, perhaps even a towel. But she wasn't. Instead she was sitting on a lounge chair, cradling Astrid.

"You gave me such a scare, Astrid. Naughty girl." She rubbed her nose against the cat's. Astrid purred softly, snuggling against her.

*What about me?* Ben wanted to ask, pulling himself out of the pool. He squeezed the bottom of his wet T-shirt and pushed his wet hair off his forehead. *Don't I get a kiss?*

The girl looked up and blinked at Ben, as if seeing him for the first time. "Oh, you're soaking wet." Astrid stared at Ben and hissed. At that moment, Ben felt like hissing back. He was scratched, sore, and soaking wet. Some way to make an impression on a girl he'd just met.

"You better get out of those clothes and dry off," she said.

With those final words, she picked up Astrid and headed into her bungalow. The door slammed shut behind her.

Ben stared after her, speechless. That was it? No thank-you? No questions to see how he was feeling? To see if maybe he'd broken something when he'd fallen from the tree? Ben shook his head. Why was he surprised? She was just like all the other girls at this hotel. Rich, spoiled, and self-centered. All she'd been worried about was her stupid cat and now that Astrid was safe and sound, he didn't matter anymore.

But what really bugged Ben was that he still didn't know her name.

He thought maybe they'd chat for a bit, introduce themselves. Now the opportunity was gone.

Of course, if he really wanted to, he could find out her name. All he'd have to do is ask Ashley at the front desk and she could tell him who the bungalow was registered to. But who was he kidding? There was no way a girl spending her summer at the South-vale Swim and Sun Club would be interested in a guy like him. They came from two different worlds. Besides, she'd just shown him what she was really like. It would be better to forget all about her.

But there was no way to forget that smile. Or those sparkling green eyes.

Ben sighed, pushing her face out of his mind. He walked back to the bungalow he had been cleaning, his wet sneakers squishing all the way. She was right about one thing: He had to get out of these clothes.

Back in the bungalow, Ben dried himself off with a towel. Finding a white terry-cloth robe behind the bathroom door, he took off his clothes and slipped into it. He'd take his wet things down to the hotel laundry room and pop them into a dryer. Then he could get dressed again and finish his cleaning.

He was on his way out of the bungalow when suddenly there was a knock on the door. Wondering who it was, he opened it.

And was taken by surprise.

It was the girl from next door.

"Hi," she said with a bright smile. "Mind if I come in?"

Ben held the door open wider. "Sure."

*What's she doing here?* Ben wondered.

"You must think I'm completely rude," she explained, stepping inside. "I was so worried about Astrid, I didn't even get a chance to thank you for getting her out of that tree."

Hearing those words, Ben's heart leaped. His first impression of her had been wrong! She wasn't like the other girls here.

"That's okay," Ben said.

"Well, I felt bad about it and I wanted to say thanks."

"You're welcome," Ben said.

The girl laughed. "What you did was really nice. I appreciate it."

"Anytime," Ben answered.

"Don't tell Astrid that."

"Why don't you get her declawed?" Ben suggested. "That way she wouldn't be climbing up trees."

The second the words were out of his mouth, Ben realized he'd said the wrong thing. The girl's eyes narrowed.

"Declaw Astrid?" she shrieked. "How cruel! A cat without claws is defenseless. I could never let her go outside."

Ben shrugged his shoulders. "Then keep her inside."

"I can't. She likes running around."

"And snacking on birds," Ben remarked. "There was a nest on the branch above the one Astrid was perched on. You should have seen the way she was eyeing the baby birds inside it."

"Astrid would never hurt another living thing," the girl said.

Ben raised an eyebrow and held out his scratched finger.

"Obviously you're not a cat person," she sniffed. "Don't worry, Ben. If Astrid climbs up another tree, I won't call you to get her down."

Ben's mouth dropped open in shock. "How do you know my name?" he asked. "I didn't tell it to you."

The girl rolled her eyes. "From your initials."

"My initials?"

"Monogrammed on the front of your robe." She pointed them out. "B.H. For Benjamin Holt."

Ben looked down and saw the burgundy initials she was pointing to. He hadn't even noticed them when he'd put on the robe. They were the same as his. But why had she called him Benjamin Holt?

"My cousin Ryan told me your family might be vacationing here this summer," she explained. "He said I should introduce myself. He told me you were a nice guy."

"Your cousin Ryan?" Ben asked, trying not to sound too confused.

"Ryan Madison. He goes to your boarding school, Bennington Academy. I'm his cousin, Lexie."

Ben nodded his head, trying to keep track of what Lexie was saying.

Lexie sighed. "I guess he didn't tell you about me. Figures. The only person Ryan likes talking about is himself."

*She thinks I'm someone else,* Ben realized. *She doesn't know that I work here. That I clean hotel rooms. She thinks I'm a guest just like she is. She thinks I'm Benjamin Holt, whoever he is.*

He had to correct Lexie's mistake. Tell her the truth. Ben opened his mouth, but before he could say anything, Lexie overrode him.

"I'm running late. I'm meeting some girlfriends for lunch." She slipped around Ben and opened the bungalow door. "Thanks again for rescuing Astrid. Maybe we'll see each other down on the beach this summer."

She waved good-bye and hurried outside, leaving a stunned Ben behind.

# Chapter 4

"*You're* interested in a girl?" Ray started laughing hysterically. It was a week later, and Ben had just told him about Lexie.

"What's so funny?" Ben asked.

"You've never been interested in a girl before. You've always been busy with a million other things." Ray flopped down on Ben's bed, clutching his sides. "I don't believe it! Ben Harris has finally been hit by Cupid's arrow!"

"Can't a guy change?" Ben grumbled.

"Sure," Ray answered. "I guess she must be something pretty special."

"Who's special?" Dougie asked, walking into Ben's bedroom. "Whatcha guys talking about?"

Ben jerked his thumb in the direction of the door. "Beat it, squirt. Out of my room."

"Looks like your brother might have a girlfriend, short stuff," Ray revealed.

"A girlfriend? To hug and kiss?" Dougie wrinkled his nose as if he'd smelled something bad. "Yuck!"

"I thought I told you to beat it," Ben said.

Dougie held out a hand. "Only if you give me some money for ice cream."

"If it means getting rid of you." Ben reached into his jeans and handed his brother a dollar. "Now scram."

"Only a buck? Some big spender you are. Saving it all for your sweetie?" Dougie started making kissing noises. "Ben's got a girlfriend. Ben's got a girlfriend."

"You're dead!" Ben shouted, charging after Dougie, who ran shrieking from the bedroom and down the stairs. A second later the front door slammed shut. When Ben returned to his bedroom, he found Ray laughing again.

"You should have seen the look on your face when Dougie started making those kissing noises." Ray started imitating Dougie's chant. "Ben's got a girlfriend. Ben's got a girlfriend."

Ben bopped Ray with a pillow. "Glad you find this all so funny."

Ray snatched the pillow out of Ben's hand and swatted him back. "Come on, Ben. I'm only teasing. I think it's great that you've found someone. Tell me about her."

"Seriously?"

Ray nodded his head. "Seriously."

"Her name is Lexie," Ben began. "I met her at the hotel."

"Is she a waitress?"

Ben shook his head as he pulled out the chair behind his desk. He turned the chair backward and sat down, leaning his arms over its back. "No. She's a guest."

"And you like her?" Ray exclaimed. "I thought you said all the girls who didn't work at the hotel were snotty and stuck-up."

"They are. But she's not. She's different."

"How can you tell?" Ray asked.

"We talked for a little bit."

"Did you ask her out?"

"No."

"How come? I thought you were nuts about her."

"There's a small problem," Ben stated.

"What?"

"She doesn't know I work at the hotel."

"How can she not know?" Ray asked. "Didn't you meet her there?"

Ben nodded. "Yes. But she thinks I'm a guest."

Ray gave Ben a confused look. "I think I'm missing something. You met her at the hotel, but she doesn't know you work there? Maybe you better go back to the beginning and fill in all the blanks."

Ben quickly told Ray the story of how he had saved Lexie's cat. "Everything happened so fast," Ben finished, "I didn't have a chance to set things straight."

"At least your story makes sense now," Ray said. He was silent for a minute. "Can I give you some advice?"

"Sure."

"We've been best friends since we were five years old. I wouldn't be saying this unless I thought you needed to hear it."

"I know."

"You don't stand a chance with her," Ray stated.

"What!" Ben jumped out of his chair. "How can you say something like that?"

"Easy. From what you've told me about the girls at this club, only one thing matters to them."

"What?" Ben demanded.

"Money," Ray stated. "And that's something you don't have."

"Money doesn't matter to Lexie."

"How can you say that?" Ray asked. "You

only talked to her for a couple of minutes. You don't even know her!"

"Neither do you," Ben shot back.

"Then how do you know I'm not right?"

Ben shrugged. "It's a feeling I have. I can't explain it, but there's something different about her. She's not like the other girls at the club."

"She was nice to you because she thought you were just like she was. Rich," Ray explained. "How do you think she'd react if she knew you were the guy who made her bed every morning?" Ray didn't wait for Ben to answer. "She'd give you the brush-off."

"No, she wouldn't," Ben insisted.

"Then what's the problem?" Ray asked. "If she's as great as you say she is, your job shouldn't make a difference. You tell her the truth and ask her out on a date. Case closed."

"I'm going to do both those things," Ben agreed. "But not in that order."

Ray sighed. "You're losing me again. What are you talking about?"

"The club is going to have a dance next Saturday night," Ben revealed. "I'm going to ask Lexie if she wants to go."

"And when are you going to tell her you clean hotel rooms?" Ray asked sarcastically.

"After she kisses you good night? Hey, maybe you'll get lucky like Cinderella and a fairy godmother will make all your wishes come true." Ray paused. "Or would that be a fairy godfather in your case?"

Ben ignored Ray's wisecrack. "I'll tell Lexie the truth. Eventually. But if pretending to be something I'm not is what it takes for her to get to know me better, then that's what I'll do first."

"What are you going to do?"

"Be rich," Ben stated simply.

"How are you planning to do that?" Ray asked. "By robbing a bank?"

"No. Something much easier. I'm going to pretend to be someone else."

"Who?"

"Someone rich." Ben's eyes lit up. "I'm going to be Benjamin Holt."

"Are you crazy?" Ray exclaimed. He jumped off Ben's bed. "That's the stupidest thing I ever heard."

"What's so stupid about it?" Ben asked. "Don't you see? Lexie thinks I'm this guy who goes to boarding school with her cousin. All I have to do is pretend to be him. Lexie and I will get to know each other and then I'll tell her the truth. She'll understand."

Ray rolled his eyes. "Understand that you've lied to her? Pretended to be someone you're not? You're taking a big risk, Ben. Girls hate being lied to. Take it from one who knows."

"I wasn't dating two girls at the same time," Ben reminded him. "And I'm not doing it for a bad reason. I'm doing it because I like her!"

"Isn't there a small problem with your plan?" Ray asked.

"I don't think so," Ben bragged. "It seems pretty foolproof to me."

"What about the *real* Ben Holt? What if he suddenly decides to check in?"

"Ashley at the front desk can keep me posted on when he's supposed to arrive with his family," Ben explained. "And that might not even happen. Gladys told me they may not use their bungalow this summer."

Ray crossed his arms over his chest. "Okay, smart guy. Since you seem to have all the answers, answer this question. What are you going to wear to the dance?"

For once, Ben was speechless. Clothes weren't exactly his specialty and most of his wardrobe consisted of T-shirts, jeans, khakis, and flannel shirts. For the Junior Prom, he'd turned down his mom's offer to

buy a suit. Why bother? He hadn't had a
date. Instead, he'd gone in a Hawaiian shirt,
shorts, and sandals.

"I hadn't thought of that," Ben admitted.

"You aren't exactly into dressing up and
those rich guys have a particular style," Ray
pointed out. "Very preppy and expensive. If
you're going to play the part, you're going
to have to look it."

Ben snapped his fingers. "I've got it.
There's a closet full of clothes in Ben Holt's
bungalow. His family shipped a bunch of
things out at the beginning of the summer.
I'm sure Ben wouldn't mind if I borrowed a
few things."

Ray shook his head. "I don't think that's a
good idea, Ben."

"Why not? Who's going to know? After I
finish wearing them, I'll put them back. No
big deal."

Ben checked the time on his watch.
"Come on. We can drive over to Southvale
and check out Ben's closet."

Ray followed Ben out of his bedroom.
"You know, I hate to be the voice of gloom
and doom, but there's one thing you haven't
thought of."

"What's that?"

"What happens when you tell Lexie the

truth and she *doesn't* understand. What then?"

"Then I'll be wrong and you'll be right," Ben said softly. "But that's not going to happen, Ray."

"Why not?"

"I won't let it," Ben vowed. "Because I'm going to sweep Lexie right off her feet."

# Chapter 5

"Am I a genius or what?" Ben exclaimed, modeling the white pants and navy blazer he'd taken out of Ben Holt's closet. "They're a perfect fit!"

"You're right," Ray grudgingly agreed. "Can we go now?"

"What's your problem?" Ben asked. "You've been jumping out of your skin ever since we got here."

"I'm nervous," Ray stated. "Isn't this trespassing?"

"How can it be trespassing? I work here!"

"Yeah, but you cleaned this bungalow hours ago," Ray pointed out. "We shouldn't be here. What if someone catches us?"

"Chill out, Ray." Ben stared at an array of conservative ties on a tie rack attached to the inside of the closet door. "None of these is really my style. Do you think I could get away with wearing one of my Looney Tunes ties?"

Ray gave Ben a skeptical look. "Get real."

"Maybe I can go without a tie."

Ray walked around the bungalow, admiring his surroundings. There was a kitchen filled with modern appliances, a living room decorated with plush furniture and a high-tech stereo and television, two bathrooms, and two bedrooms. On his way back to the living room, he stuck his head in the refrigerator and was disappointed to find it empty.

"This place is swanky," Ray remarked. "It's almost like a house."

Ben scooped his shorts and T-shirt off the bedroom floor and went into the bathroom to change. "Check out the TV," he called out. "It gets over seventy-five channels."

Ray flopped down on the sofa and pointed the remote control at the TV, flicking through channels. "What's next?"

"Why don't we go to the front desk and meet Ashley?"

Ray perked up at the suggestion. "Is she a babe?"

Ben emerged from the bathroom with the pants and blazer on a hanger. He put them back into the closet in Ben Holt's bedroom and returned to the living room. "I guess so. She's pretty. And very sweet."

"So why don't you go out with her? It would make your life much easier."

"I don't want to go out with Ashley. I want to go out with Lexie."

Ray flicked off the TV and jumped to his feet. He ran a finger across the top of a painting on the wall and then studied it. "No dust. I'm impressed."

"All the rooms I clean would pass the white glove test," Ben bragged.

"Are we finished here?" Ray asked.

"Almost," Ben said.

Ray raised an eyebrow. "*Almost?*"

"I just had another idea."

"No," Ray answered, folding his arms over his chest. "N-O. No."

"But you haven't even heard what it is!"

"I'm not going to like it," Ray stated. "Trust me. I haven't liked any of the ideas you've come up with today."

Ben waved his arms around at the bungalow. "No one's staying here. I'll bet if I wanted to use this place, I could."

"You mean stay here overnight?"

"Or hang out during the day."

"So you could maybe catch a glimpse of Lexie when she's leaving her bungalow and *accidentally* bump into her?"

"Uh-huh," Ben confirmed.

"Couldn't you get fired if your boss finds out? I mean, it *isn't* your bungalow," Ray reminded. "Just like the clothes in that closet aren't yours."

"I'm not going to do it all summer. Maybe once or twice. And it's not like I'm stealing the clothes in Ben Holt's closet. I told you before. I'm only borrowing them."

"The only thing you're going to do is dig yourself into a deeper hole."

"I am not," Ben said.

"Don't do it, Ben," Ray advised.

"One time," Ben said. "That's all."

"Don't do it," Ray repeated. "Trust me. You could get yourself into a lot of trouble."

"You worry too much," Ben said. "Come on, let's go meet Ashley."

They left the bungalow and walked along a pebbled path shaded with palm trees. The intense heat of the blazing July sun was like a thick woolen blanket, heavy and hot, and they eagerly stepped into the air-conditioned coolness of the hotel lobby.

"There's Ashley," Ben pointed out, wiping a bead of sweat off his forehead.

Ray looked where Ben was pointing. "That's Ashley?"

Ben nodded his head.

"Are you sure you wouldn't rather go out with her than Lexie?"

"Yes, I'm sure," Ben answered.

"Positive?" Ray asked.

"Yes, yes, yes," Ben said. "Why do you keep asking?"

Ray checked himself out in a mirror, running a hand through his curls and smoothing his wrinkled T-shirt. "I just want to make sure you're not interested because I really like what I'm seeing."

"Want an introduction?"

Ray made a face at Ben. "Have I ever needed your help meeting a girl?"

Ben made a face back. "Excu-u-u-use me!" With Ray trailing behind him, Ben walked over to the front desk. "Hi, Ashley."

Ashley looked up from the keyboard she was typing on. "Hi, Ben. Who's your friend?"

Ray waved a hand. "Hey, I'm Ray."

"You don't work at the hotel, do you? I've never seen you around."

"I work at Dog Gone Clean. It's a pet grooming shop in Berkley Heights. You got a dog or cat that needs sprucing up? I could get you a discount."

"Thanks, but I don't have any pets. I'm allergic."

"Bummer."

Figuring he'd given Ray enough time to work his charms, Ben interrupted. "Listen, Ash. I wanted to ask a favor. Do you think you could let me know when the Holts are going to be checking in? I've been cleaning their bungalow every day and I've started slacking off a little. Nothing really needs to be done, you know? But I want to make sure the place is in tip-top shape before they show up."

Ashley turned to her keyboard and hit a few keys. She stared at her computer screen. "According to the file, they're still not scheduled to arrive. If anything changes, I'll let you know."

"Thanks."

"Are you going to the dance next Saturday?" she asked.

"I thought I'd swing by. You?"

Ashley nodded her head. "I'll be there. How about you, Ray? You like dancing?"

"I could get into it."

"Maybe I'll see you there."

The phone lines on Ashley's desk started ringing and she began answering them.

"I think Ashley likes you," Ben commented as they walked away. "You going to come to the dance?"

"You bet. But not because Ashley kind of invited me."

"Then why are you going?"

"No way am I going to miss your imper-sonation of Benjamin Holt." Ray followed Ben out of the hotel and back outside. "What do you want to do now?"

"Want to check out the beach?"

"Any particular reason?" Ray prodded.

"No."

"Liar. I've seen your eyes scanning the hotel. You're searching for Lexie."

"What if I am?" Ben admitted.

"You think she might be on the beach?"

"Only one way to find out."

Ben and Ray walked down to the beach. Once they hit the white sand, they took off their T-shirts and sandals.

"Ow! Hot," Ray complained.

Ben grabbed Ray's arm. "There she is."

Ray shaded his eyes from the sun, jump-ing from one foot to the other as he put his sandals back on. "Where?"

Ben pointed. "Sitting under that blue-and-white-striped beach umbrella."

Ray whistled. "Wow. You were right, Ben. She's a knockout."

Ben punched Ray lightly on the arm. "I told you so."

Ben hurried over to Lexie's spot on the beach while Ray tagged behind. She was sitting on a white beach blanket, reading a magazine. Her hair was piled on top of her head, held up with a red ribbon, and she was wearing a red bikini with white polka dots.

Too busy reading her magazine, she didn't notice Ben at first. Then she glanced up and lowered her sunglasses. It was the chance Ben was waiting for.

"Hi," he said, giving her a smile.

"Hi." Lexie stared blankly at Ben. "I'm sorry. I know we've met before, but I can't remember your name."

She didn't remember him! Ben was crushed. How could she have forgotten him so quickly? It had only been a week since he'd rescued her cat.

"I'm Ben. Ben Holt."

Ben was surprised at how easily the words slipped past his lips. Except for a few white lies, he'd never lied before. At least not in such a *major* way. Was it always such a snap?

"That's right!" Lexie exclaimed. "You rescued Astrid from the tree. Sorry. I'm such a space cadet when it comes to remembering names. I haven't seen you around much."

"I've been kind of busy."

Lexie nodded her head, taking a sip of her diet Coke. "Me too."

"Are you going to the dance next Saturday?"

Lexie thought about Ben's question for a second. "I'm not sure. Maybe." She opened a bottle of suntan oil and rubbed some into her arms. "If there's nothing better to do."

Ben could smell the sweet scent of coconut as Lexie rubbed the oil into her tanned arms. "Would you mind getting my back?" she asked, holding out the bottle. "I always have a hard time."

Ben couldn't believe his ears. Ever since last week he'd been wondering what it would be like to hold Lexie in his arms and now he was getting a chance at the next best thing.

"Sure," he said.

But before Ben could kneel behind Lexie on her blanket and begin spreading the oil over her back, a girl in a one-piece navy blue swimsuit dashed up to the blanket. "Hey, Lexie. Are you up for a volleyball game?"

Lexie tossed down her magazine and jumped to her feet. "Am I ever!" She gave Ben a wave, running after her friend. " 'Bye!"

Ray joined Ben's side as Lexie disappeared over a sand dune and out of sight. He'd kept his distance, giving Ben enough space to make his move with Lexie, but he'd been close enough to overhear their conversation.

"She doesn't even know you're alive," Ray announced. He didn't want to hurt his friend's feelings, but there was nothing else he could say.

"That's not true," Ben said.

"She didn't even ask if you were going to the dance," Ray pointed out.

"She would have."

"She ditched you for a volleyball game," Ray stated. "And she didn't remember your name."

"But she asked me to put suntan oil on her back," Ben threw back.

"That's not something to brag about," Ray said. "Maybe you ought to forget about Lexie and give Ashley a chance."

"I told you, I'm not interested in Ashley."

Ray threw up his hands in surrender. "Okay. But what happens next?"

"I don't know," Ben admitted. "My timing with Lexie has been off. I guess I'll go to the dance next Saturday and hope she shows up."

# Chapter 6

"You're going to the dance dressed like *that*?" Ben exclaimed.

"What's wrong with the way I'm dressed?" Ray asked, stepping into Ben's bungalow.

"You look like you're getting ready to bale hay," Ben said.

"Har. Har."

"I'm serious," Ben stated. Instead of dressing up for the dance, Ray had chosen to dress down. He was wearing a pair of denim overalls with a lime green T-shirt underneath. On his feet were a pair of purple sneakers with neon green laces. "You're going to stick out like a sore thumb."

"So? What's the big deal?"

"Maybe we can find something in Ben's closet that will fit you." Ben grabbed Ray's arm and pulled him in the direction of the bedroom, but Ray snatched his arm free.

"I don't want to change my clothes. What's your problem, Ben?" he complained. "There's no dress code for the dance. A couple of months ago this is the way *you* would have dressed for a dance."

"But this isn't a couple of months ago. This is now. Tonight. We're hanging out with a totally different group."

Ray threw up his hands in surrender. "Hey, if you want to pretend to be someone you're not, that's fine. But not me. This is who I am. What's the matter, Ben? Ashamed to be seen with me? Afraid that I'll give you away?"

"Of course not," Ben said. "But don't you want to fit in?"

"With who? I don't care if these guys like me. I'm just here to have fun. You used to be the same way, Ben. You never used to care what people thought."

"I care what Lexie thinks," Ben stated.

"That's the problem!" Ray exclaimed. "Everything you do these days revolves around Lexie. I know you're crazy about her, but I wish you'd never met her. She's really messing with your head."

"She is not."

"Yes, she is," Ray argued. "She's got you

doing things you wouldn't ordinarily do. Like using this bungalow."

"I told you it would be easier if I changed my clothes here," Ben explained. "It's only for tonight. I didn't think it would be right to take Ben's clothes to my house."

"Whatever," Ray said, heading for the front door.

"Where are you going?"

"I'm outta here. But don't worry, I won't blow your cover at the dance tonight. I'll pretend not to know you. It shouldn't be too hard. You're becoming just as thoughtless and self-centered as those snobs you want to hang out with. Catch you later."

Ben watched Ray leave the bungalow. He could see he'd hurt his friend's feelings, but he hadn't done it intentionally. Why couldn't Ray understand that he was nervous about tonight? He wanted everything to go off without a hitch.

Maybe it was better this way. After all, would the real Benjamin Holt hang out with someone dressed in overalls and purple sneakers? In the future, he'd be sure not to involve Ray with Lexie. He'd keep the two parts of his life separate. It would make things less complicated.

With Ray gone, Ben concentrated on getting dressed. He took a shower in the bathroom and then slipped into the clothes he'd selected from Ben's closet: white pants, navy jacket, and blue shirt. No tie. He even found a pair of loafers that had a fancy gold crest on their front.

After getting dressed, Ben positioned himself by a window, peeking through the curtains. He could see a light on in Lexie's bungalow. Should he go next door and knock? But what if she wasn't going to the dance? Maybe he should wait until she left and then follow her. They could meet on their way inside.

Outside, Ben could hear voices. He turned his head to the left and saw two girls walking up the path to Lexie's bungalow. One was the girl in the navy swimsuit who'd asked Lexie to play volleyball. She was tall, wearing a short black dress with thin straps. Her red hair was worn in a French twist.

The girl walking next to her was shorter. Her dark brown hair was shoulder-length, pushed back with a white headband. She wore a yellow sundress decorated with daisies.

The door to Lexie's bungalow opened. Ben tried to catch a glimpse of Lexie but couldn't. The girls quickly stepped inside and the door closed.

They had to be going to the dance. Why else would they be all dressed up? But what if he was wrong? What if they were headed somewhere else? Should he follow them? That way if they weren't going to the dance, he could go wherever they were going. But what if they were headed to a private party?

Ben watched Lexie's bungalow until the lights went out. Then he hurried to the front door. Opening the door a crack, he peeked outside. It was getting dark. The sun was gone and the lights lining the hotel paths hadn't come on yet. He couldn't see Lexie, but her two friends were following her. All three were talking and laughing.

Ben slipped out of the bungalow, making sure the door locked behind him. He decided to follow Lexie and her friends. If they went to the dance, great. If not, he'd hope he could get in wherever they were going.

Ben gave a sigh of relief when they walked past the hotel parking lot. That meant they were going to the dance.

Inside the hotel, Lexie and her friends headed in the direction of the ladies' room. Ben still hadn't gotten a glimpse of her. He wondered what she was wearing. He walked into the ballroom where the dance was taking place. He hoped he would see her soon and be able to catch her by herself. It would be much easier talking to her alone than with her friends around.

Ben was impressed with the decorations for the dance. The ballroom had been transformed into a Hawaiian paradise. Colorful paper flowers in a variety of colors were strung across the room and there were palm trees filled with coconuts.

A buffet table was spread out in a corner. There was a roasted pig with an apple stuck in its mouth, barbecued ribs, and lots of pineapple. Waitresses in flowered skirts carried trays filled with exotic-looking drinks and ukulele players wearing bright Hawaiian shirts strummed their instruments for girls in grass skirts doing the hula.

Across the ballroom, Ben could see Ray talking with Ashley. She looked cute in a flowered skirt and white halter top. She waved and Ben waved back. Ray ignored him.

Ben didn't let Ray's snub bother him. By tomorrow they'd be talking again. Ray would cool off and they'd patch things up. They always did.

Ben turned his eyes back to the entrance of the ballroom, searching for Lexie. He didn't want to miss her.

Fifteen minutes later, there was still no sign of Lexie. Ben began moving through the ballroom. Could she have come in without him seeing her?

Ben was on his way to the punch bowl when he bumped into someone. It was a girl in a lacy violet dress, holding a glass of punch. Some of it spilled to the floor.

"I'm sorry," Ben apologized, reaching for a napkin. "I hope I didn't spill any on you."

The girl turned around and Ben's breath caught in his throat. It was Lexie. And she looked beautiful.

"Hi, Ben! See, I remembered your name this time," she teased.

Ben gave Lexie a smile, unable to take his eyes off her. For the first time since he'd met her, she was wearing her hair down. It shimmered in the soft light of the ballroom, falling past her shoulders in cascading waves. She wore hardly any makeup except for some lipstick and her skin glowed from being out in the sun. She looked fantastic.

"Have you met my friends?" she asked.

Ben turned his eyes to the two girls standing behind Lexie.

"This is Dionne," Lexie introduced, pointing first to the tall redhead and then to the girl in the daisy sundress. "And this is Pam."

Ben smiled at both girls, but neither one smiled back. Ben immediately knew the score with them. They were the kind of girls who thought they were better than everyone else because they were pretty and popular. They got invited to all the right parties, belonged to all the right clubs, and could have any boyfriend they wanted.

They didn't like him. He could sense it. And until they knew more about him, they weren't going to change their feelings.

"Where did you and Lexie meet?" Dionne asked.

"I told you the story," Lexie reminded her. "He rescued Astrid from a tree. He's staying in the bungalow next to mine."

Pam munched on a slice of dried apricot. "I wish this dance was more exclusive," she complained. "Hotel employees and people who don't belong to the club shouldn't be allowed to attend. Look at that slob in the corner."

Pam was pointing at Ray. "Did he just roll out of bed?"

"He looks pretty comfortable to me," Ben offered. "Sometimes a tie can make you feel strangled."

"Someone should use one to strangle him," Pam said.

"Where do you go to school?" Dionne asked.

"He goes to Bennington Academy with my cousin Ryan," Lexie said.

"I've been to dances at Bennington Academy," Dionne said, studying Ben. "I've never seen you there."

Ben shrugged his shoulders. "Must have been one of those times when I went home for the weekend," he answered, hoping he didn't sound nervous.

"This dance is really lame," Pam complained.

"Absolutely dead," Dionne agreed.

"There aren't even any cute guys," Pam added. "Why don't we get your car, Lexie, and go cruising around?"

"Okay," Lexie answered. "I'll meet you guys out front."

Pam and Dionne left without saying good-bye to Ben. He couldn't care less. But Lexie was leaving and he'd hardly said two words to her! This always happened. What was the problem?

"Are you sure you don't want to stay?" Ben rushed to ask. He didn't want her to leave. He wanted her to stay. But how could he do that? "It's still early."

Lexie shook her head. "Nah. Pam and Dionne are right. It's too quiet."

Ben wondered what to say next. Maybe he should agree with her. Maybe then she'd invite him to tag along. Or maybe he should invite himself.

"Have fun," Lexie said, walking away.

Ben watched as Lexie weaved her way through the party crowd. Everywhere he looked, people were having a good time. Even Ray, who was doing the limbo with Ashley and another girl who worked at the hotel.

Feeling sorry for himself, Ben decided to drown his sorrows in a glass of punch. He had just placed the glass to his lips when his arm was suddenly grabbed. Some of his drink spilled to the floor.

Ben whirled around with an annoyed look on his face, but it disappeared when he saw who it was.

Lexie.

"Quick!" she ordered. "Dance with me."

Without giving Ben a chance to say anything, Lexie threw herself into his arms.

# Chapter 7

Ben was taken completely by surprise.

"You can dance, can't you?" Lexie asked.

Ben nodded his head, too tongue-tied to answer because the girl of his dreams was in his arms.

"Then don't just stand there; start moving your feet!"

Ben whisked Lexie out onto the dance floor. The band had started playing a slow, romantic song. Couples were holding each other close, nuzzling cheeks and whispering in each other's ears. Some were even kissing. Ben didn't think he'd be able to do any of that with Lexie — at least, not so soon — so he started talking to her.

"I thought the dance was too quiet for you."

"Can't a girl change her mind?"

"Sure," Ben agreed. "But there's usually a reason."

"No reason."

Ben gave Lexie a skeptical look. "You mean you suddenly had an irresistible urge to dance?"

"I like this song."

"Really?" Ben asked. "It's ancient. Where'd you hear it?" he challenged.

"An old Audrey Hepburn movie I caught on the late show." Lexie peered over Ben's shoulder and then gave him a smile. "Can we not talk and just dance?"

Ben gazed into Lexie's eyes. For the first time, he noticed flecks of gold mixed with the green. He studied the rest of her face more closely. It was perfect. She really was the most beautiful girl he'd ever met.

Lexie's lips were only inches away from Ben's. As he stared at them, he was suddenly tempted. Tempted to kiss her.

"Ben? Are you all right?"

Ben gave Lexie an embarrassed smile. "Guess I spaced out."

Lexie moved closer to Ben and rested her head on his shoulder. He could smell the strawberry scent of her shampoo, as well as the perfume she was wearing. He'd never smelled anything sweeter.

A few minutes later, Lexie moved her head from Ben's shoulder. He was disappointed, but at least he was still holding her in his arms.

As they danced, Ben noticed something. Lexie kept looking over his shoulder. It was almost as if she were searching for someone. When he had the chance, he followed her gaze.

On the edge of the dance floor he saw a dark-haired guy. There was no mistaking the scowl on his face as he stared in Lexie's direction. He wasn't happy seeing her dance with another guy.

Suddenly Ben realized what was going on — why Lexie was in such a rush to dance with him. His heart plummeted.

"What's the matter?" Lexie asked. "You look sad."

"Can I ask you a question?"

Lexie gave Ben a coy smile. "It depends on the question."

"Are you using me?" Ben asked bluntly.

Lexie's eyes widened with shock. Then they filled with hurt.

"I would never do anything like that!" she cried.

"Really?" Ben jerked his thumb across the dance floor. "Then who's that guy watching us? If looks could kill, I'd be dead."

"That's Joel," Lexie said.

"Are you trying to make him jealous?" Ben asked.

"No way," Lexie stated. "I can't stand him!"

Lexie's answer threw Ben off guard. "Then why do you want him to see us together? Don't deny it, Lexie. I've seen you peeking over my shoulder at him. I'm confused. Gimme a little help."

"I didn't think you'd notice," Lexie admitted guiltily.

"It wasn't hard to do. You were pretty obvious."

Lexie took a deep breath. "It's a long story, but I'll try to give you the basics. Joel's my ex-boyfriend. We dated last spring."

"Why'd you break up?"

"He dumped me for someone else."

Ben couldn't believe Lexie's answer. How could Joel dump Lexie for someone else? What a jerk!

"I'm sorry."

"Don't be. It was the best thing that ever happened to me. Joel liked to boss me around. Tell me what to do. I like making my own decisions."

"Why do you want him to see us together?"

"I want him to see that I'm happy without him. After we broke up, I tried to get back together with him. I really made a fool of myself until I realized he wasn't worth it."

"There had to be a reason why you wanted to get back together with him. Did you love him?"

"I thought I did. At the time. Then I realized I didn't. It's hard to explain, but I didn't *feel* it. You know what I mean?"

"I think I do," Ben answered. "When you fall in love with someone, you know it immediately. Instinctively. I don't think you can deny it. You just *know* you're in love."

"Exactly!" Lexie agreed. "So far that hasn't happened to me, but when I fall in love for the first time, I'm going to know it."

*I already do,* Ben wanted to say. Instead, he asked, "If Joel's dating someone else, why should he care who you're seeing?"

"Joel broke up with his new girlfriend and now he wants to get back together with me," Lexie explained. "When he called me up a couple of days ago, I told him to get lost."

"And he didn't?"

Lexie shook her head. "Joel likes a challenge. Because I wouldn't go running back to him, he's determined to win me back. No one says no to him."

"Except you."

Lexie smiled. "Except me."

The music ended and the band started playing a disco tune from the seventies. The dance floor filled with new couples while other couples left.

"Want to dance again?" Ben asked. He started imitating John Travolta from *Saturday Night Fever.* "I left my white suit at home, but I can do the moves."

Lexie started laughing but then stopped. She grabbed Ben's hand and pulled him in the direction of the terrace. "Let's go outside."

Ben turned around and saw Joel headed their way. "Lexie, you can't run away from him."

"I can try!" she exclaimed.

They slipped out onto the terrace and found a spot hidden behind some potted palms. A cool breeze was blowing and the scent of salt water wafted from the beach.

*She's using me. Again,* Ben thought. *But I don't care. As long as I can still be with her, I don't care.*

"This is nice," Lexie said, leaning against

the white terrace railing. "It was starting to get hot in there."

"You're changing the subject," Ben pointed out.

"So what if I am?"

"How long until he finds us?"

"Let's not talk about Joel," Lexie pleaded.

Ben joined Lexie against the railing. "How's your summer going?" he asked.

"I'm going crazy cooped up in this place. It's like a prison."

"It's not that bad."

"Not if you'd rather be someplace else," Lexie grumbled.

"Where would you rather be?"

"Backpacking across Europe," she said wistfully.

"How come you're not?"

"My parents don't think I'm old enough." Lexie rolled her eyes. "I don't know how your parents are, but mine really drive me crazy sometimes. It's like they don't know who I am and they don't want to know."

Ben frowned. "What do you mean?"

"They want me to be a carbon copy of them."

"Is that bad?"

"Yes! The only thing that matters to my family is money. My dad is a lawyer, charging three hundred dollars an hour. My mom is an interior designer. She charges two hundred dollars an hour. My two older sisters are in college and they want to be lawyers like my dad. All they care about is how much money they can make and how it can be turned into more."

"Do you live in Southvale?" Ben asked.

"Yes, but my family is building a new house. Until it's ready, I'm staying here. How about you? Do you live in Southvale?"

Ben panicked. Did Benjamin Holt live in Southvale? He didn't know! "I do for the summer," he answered, hoping Lexie wouldn't ask for more details. He quickly changed the subject. "I guess you're not going to be a lawyer when you graduate from college."

"No way!" Lexie exclaimed.

"What do you want to do?"

"I'd like to be a street artist," Lexie revealed. "You know, the type that sketches your picture. Wouldn't it be wild to live in New Orleans or Paris and sketch all day? I wouldn't do it forever. Just for a couple of years. Then I'd come home and be an art teacher. I love to draw and I love kids."

"Sounds like fun."

"My parents don't think so," Lexie said.

"They nearly had a heart attack when I told them. They said I wouldn't be able to support myself. Who cares? Life's an adventure, right? You see where it takes you. I want to experience the world and try new things."

Ben agreed with everything Lexie had said. He wanted to see the world after he graduated from college, too. Before he could say anything, a voice cut him off.

"So this is where you disappeared to!" Dionne exclaimed.

"Mind if we join the party, or is it private?" Pam asked, not waiting for an answer. She sat down on a lounge chair. "We didn't think we'd ever find you."

"Thanks so much for leaving us waiting outside," Dionne complained.

"Sorry," Lexie apologized. "I lost track of time. We can still go."

"Forget it," Dionne said. "The dance isn't so dull anymore. Guess who we ran into!"

"Who?" Lexie asked.

"Joel!" Dionne announced. She reached out behind the palm trees with a hand and Joel emerged with a smile on his face.

Ben saw Lexie's own smile disappear at the sight of Joel. Instantly he felt protective of Lexie. He wanted to go over to her and wrap an arm around her, telling her he wouldn't let Joel hurt her again.

Seeing Joel up close, Ben disliked him even more. Joel was a good-looking guy and he knew it, using those looks to get whatever he wanted. Dionne and Pam were already wrapped around his finger. He'd used them to bust in on Ben and Lexie.

"Hey, Lex," Joel said. "I've been trying to invite you to a pool party I'm throwing next Saturday. You kept hanging up on me every time I called."

"It sounds like a blast," Pam raved. "We're going to be there. You're going to come, aren't you, Lexie?"

"You wouldn't miss my party, would you, Lex?" Joel asked. "It wouldn't be any fun without you."

"She'll be there," Dionne answered. "Won't you, Lexie?"

"I can't make it," Lexie answered. "Ben and I are spending next Saturday together, aren't we, Ben?"

*We are?* Ben saw the pleading look in Lexie's eyes and immediately answered, "Yeah, we are."

"What are you doing?" Dionne asked.

"We'll probably go to the beach," Lexie answered.

"If you're going swimming," Pam said, "then why not come to Joel's?"

"Joel didn't invite Ben," Lexie pointed out.

Joel turned to Ben. He took a sip from the glass of punch in his hand. "I'd invite you if I could, Ben, but the party's being catered and we've already ordered the food."

It was the lamest excuse Ben had ever heard. Like there wouldn't be enough food for one extra person? He didn't care that Joel didn't want him at his party, but he didn't even have the guts to say it.

"Ben goes to Bennington Academy," Dionne said. "I told him I'd been to dances there and I'd never seen him before."

Joel studied Ben over the rim of his punch glass. "I've been to a couple of Bennington dances, too. I've never seen you, either."

Ben shrugged.

"Who do you hang out with?" Joel asked.

Ben gave a safe answer. "Lexie's cousin. Ryan."

"Who else?" Joel prodded.

Ben decided to keep playing it safe. That way he couldn't be tripped up by his own lies. "No one you would know."

"Try me," Joel challenged. "I know practically everybody."

Luckily, Pam saved Ben from having to answer.

"Why don't we go back inside where it's air-conditioned? I'm starting to melt out here," she exclaimed, waving a hand in front of her face.

"We're going to stay out a little longer," Lexie said.

Dionne and Pam ignored Ben again, leaving without saying good-bye. As Joel walked past Ben toward the terrace doors, he tripped, splashing his punch over the front of Ben's pants. The vivid red color of the punch stood out against Ben's white pants.

"I'm such a klutz," Joel said. "Sorry."

Ben could see Joel wasn't sorry. Dionne and Pam watched from the terrace doors, suppressing their giggles.

"He did that on purpose," Lexie said after they were gone, wiping the front of Ben's pants with a napkin.

"No kidding."

"It's not coming out."

"Don't worry about it," Ben said. "I'll wash them."

"Sorry I put you on the spot like that. It's just that I didn't want to go to Joel's pool party. I can usually handle Joel on my own, but when he teams up with Dionne and Pam, I'm outnumbered. They can really twist your arm."

"I could tell."

"If you want, we really could spend Saturday afternoon together," Lexie said.

"Do you want to?" Ben asked.

"Why not? It's better than spending the afternoon alone, hiding in my bungalow. Besides, if we didn't spend the afternoon together, it would make me a liar. And I hate liars."

Ben didn't say anything. Suddenly his conscience was screaming at him! *Tell her the truth! Tell her the truth!*

"You know something else?" Lexie asked.

"What?"

"Pam was wrong. There are cute guys at the dance. Nice ones, too. I should know. I got to dance with one."

# Chapter 8

"How much?" Ben gasped, not sure he'd heard the salesclerk correctly.

"Two hundred dollars."

"I thought that's what you said." Ben groaned.

"Guess your foolproof plan wasn't so foolproof," Ray stated as the salesclerk returned to his register.

"If you say 'I told you so' one more time . . ." Ben warned.

Last night Ben had taken Ben Holt's pants home to wash. He figured he'd toss the pants in the washing machine, the stain would come out, and he'd return them to Ben Holt's closet the next morning.

It wasn't that easy.

When he'd taken the pants out of the washer, the stain still remained, as bright and as vivid as when he'd tossed the pants in. Ben tried washing them again. And again. And again. He stayed up until three o'clock in the morning and used every box of detergent in his mom's laundry room, but the stain still remained. He'd even used a scrub brush.

At first he didn't panic, figuring a dry cleaner would be able to get the stain out. But when he'd gone to a dry cleaner that morning before heading to work, he'd been told he'd be better off throwing the pants out.

That left only one solution.

Buy a new pair of pants.

At the hotel Ben called Ray and asked if he wanted to tag along with him to the mall. If Ray said yes, Ben would know the fight they'd had last night was forgotten. If he said no, Ben would know he was still mad.

"Sure," Ray mumbled, still half asleep. "I'll meet you at four."

During his rounds at the hotel, Ben made sure to keep a low profile. Before ducking out to his cleaning cart in the hallway, he made sure the coast was clear. He didn't want anyone catching sight of him.

While he was cleaning Ben Holt's bungalow, Ben kept peeking out the window at Lexie's bungalow. He thought maybe she might be swimming in her pool with Pam and Dionne, but all was quiet. He'd saved Ben Holt's bungalow for last and after he'd finished cleaning he hung out for a while, hoping Lexie might stop by. But she didn't. He stayed until he finally had to leave to meet Ray.

At the mall Ben and Ray went to the first clothing store they found, searching for a pair of white pants with the same designer label as Ben Holt's.

Ben found the pants immediately, but his first sign of trouble was when he saw the pants were chained to the rack. The second sign of trouble was the fact that there was no price tag attached to the pants.

Not good.

When the salesclerk told Ben how much the pants were, he didn't believe him and had to ask again. Maybe he'd heard wrong.

He hadn't. The price was still the same: two hundred dollars.

"Two hundred bucks," Ray whispered. "What are you going to do?"

"I don't have much of a choice," Ben said. "The pants have to be replaced or else I'm in big trouble."

"Where are you going to get the money?"

Ben reached into his wallet and took out

his cash card. "I'm going to have to with-draw it from my savings account."

Ray's eyes bugged out. "I don't think I've ever seen you take money out of the bank. You're worse than Ebenezer Scrooge."

"What else am I supposed to do, wise guy?"

"Wait! I've got an idea. Why don't you buy a cheaper pair of pants?"

"I can't." Ben pointed to the pants on the rack. "I have to buy *those*. You don't think he'll know the difference?"

"Not if we cut off the label from the pants you ruined and sew it into the new pair," Ray said. He reached for a pair of white pants from a nearby rack and held them up. "They're practically identical." He glanced at the price tag on the pants. "And super cheap."

Ben hated to admit it, but Ray's plan was a good one. He really didn't want to dip into his college savings account. He'd been saving for years, putting away birthday money and whatever he could save from his al-lowance.

It was on the tip of his tongue to say yes. Would Ben Holt really be able to tell the dif-ference? Probably not. And his closet was bursting with clothes. There were at least two other pairs of white pants. He should just do it.

Yet in the end, Ben decided against it. Even though it would be easy to make the switch, he knew it was wrong.

"I can't," he told Ray. "It wouldn't be right."

Ben went to a cash machine out in the mall and used his cash card to make a withdrawal from his savings account. Two weeks of pay down the drain.

"That's got to hurt," Ray said.

It hurt even more when Ben had to hand the money over to the salesclerk.

"Was last night worth two hundred dollars?" Ray asked as they left the store with the pants.

"It doesn't matter how much the pants cost," Ben said as they walked outside to the parking lot. "It got me a date with Lexie."

"It's not like you have a *real* date with her," Ray pointed out. "She's just pretending so that Joel won't hassle her."

"It's a start."

"It's a pity date," Ray shot back.

"You just said it wasn't a real date. How can it be a pity date?"

"She feels sorry for you because he ruined your pants," Ray explained. "She wants to make it up to you."

"Whatever kind of date it is, it's a date," Ben said as they walked across the parking lot to his car. "The best part of all is that Lexie and I will be alone."

"What do you plan on picking her up in?"

"Huh?"

Ray pointed to Ben's dusty Dodge. "This old heap is not exactly the kind of car that Ben Holt would be driving around in. I'd say a Mercedes is more his style."

Ben slapped a hand over his eyes. He hadn't even thought about his car. It was a dead giveaway. Ray was right.

"Maybe I can rent a car," Ben suggested as they slipped into the front seat.

"No can do. You have to be twenty-five years old."

"There has to be a solution," Ben said, buckling up his seat belt.

"Know anyone who has a spare Mercedes?"

Ben was quiet for a second as he started up the car, then his face lit up. "No, but I do know someone whose father has a Corvette."

Ray's eyes widened. "No way."

"Come on, Ray," Ben pleaded. "It's only for one afternoon."

"Are you crazy? My father will kill me."

Ben pulled out of his parking space. "He'll

never know. Aren't your folks going away for the weekend?"

"Yes."

"And aren't they taking the station wagon?"

"Yes-s-s-s," Ray answered slowly.

"That means your dad's car will be sitting in the garage the entire weekend."

"What if something happens to it?"

"Nothing will happen. I swear it." Ben crossed his heart. "I'll be extra careful. Promise."

"I'd be grounded for life if anything happened to that car," Ray said.

"Nothing will happen," Ben repeated.

"Here's a compromise," Ray suggested. "You can use the car, but only if we double-date. I'll bring Ashley."

"Ray, I want to be *alone* with Lexie. How am I going to get to know her better if you and Ashley are there?"

"That's my offer. Take it or leave it."

"Ray . . ."

Ray shook his head stubbornly. "You can talk until you're blue in the face, Ben, but I'm not changing my mind. You're not borrowing my dad's car, and that's final!"

# Chapter 9

"I love your car!" Lexie raved. "It's a Corvette, isn't it?"

"From 1965," Ben answered.

Lexie walked around the fire-engine-red Corvette, admiring it. "Where did you get it?"

After much arm-twisting and pleading, along with the promise that he'd pay for Ray's next four dates with Ashley, Ben had managed to get Ray to lend him his father's car. Ben knew he couldn't tell Lexie the truth, so he stretched it.

"A birthday present." It wasn't exactly a lie. Ray's father had bought himself the car for his fortieth birthday.

"It's gorgeous."

"So are you going to hop in or just stare at it?"

"Definitely hop in," Lexie said. "I can't wait to go for a ride!"

Lexie slipped into the front seat. She was wearing faded denim shorts and a pink T-shirt knotted at the waist. Her long hair was pulled back into a ponytail and a pair of sunglasses was perched on top of her head.

Lexie slipped her sunglasses over her eyes and turned on the radio. "Where are we off to?"

Ben pulled the car out of the hotel parking lot and drove into the street. "If it's okay with you, I thought we'd skip the beach and go somewhere else."

"How come?"

"That way Pam, Dionne, and Joel can't accidentally bump into us after their pool party."

"Smart thinking." Lexie reached into her bag for a pack of gum and stuck a piece in her mouth. She offered a stick to Ben. "Then where are we going?"

Ben unwrapped his stick of gum. "A flea market."

"A flea market?" Lexie exclaimed.

"You've never been?"

"Isn't that where they sell a lot of old junk?"

"Don't call it junk. You can find really neat stuff at flea markets. It's like digging for buried treasure. It's a lot of fun."

Lexie shrugged. "If you say so."

"You'll see."

The flea market was packed when they arrived. There were rows and rows of vendors selling everything from china and glasses to lamps and furniture.

"Where do we start?" Lexie asked.

"Anywhere you want."

Lexie spied a rack of old clothes and raced over to it. She tossed a yellow feather boa around her neck and posed. "Is it me?"

Ben grabbed the end of the boa and pulled Lexie toward him. "You'd look great in anything."

Lexie fell into Ben's arms, laughing. "Thanks, but I don't think I'd have much use for this."

Even though he wanted to keep holding her, Ben reluctantly let Lexie go. He watched as she went back to searching through the rack of clothes.

For the rest of the day, Lexie got into the spirit of things, poking through trays of merchandise, asking prices, and trying to bargain — something she wasn't aware she was supposed to do.

"Part of the fun of flea markets is bargaining with the vendors," Ben explained when Lexie was willing to pay for two tortoiseshell hair combs without haggling over the price.

Lexie stared at Ben with disbelief. "You mean you don't pay the price on the ticket?"

"Not if you can help it."

Armed with those words of wisdom, Lexie went back to the vendor, prepared to do shopping battle. Besides the two tortoiseshell hair combs, Lexie also bought a silk scarf and a handmade shawl. And she got them all at a lesser price.

"Look at those Barbie dolls," Lexie said as they passed a vendor selling old toys.

"I'll bet you kept your Barbies in mint condition."

"Uh-uh. I cut all their hair off and chewed on their feet. I was a naughty little girl."

"You're not naughty anymore?"

Lexie raised an eyebrow at Ben. "That's for me to know and you to find out."

Next to the vendor selling toys was a vendor selling jewelry. Lexie rummaged through the trays of glittering necklaces, earrings, and pins on display. She stopped when her eyes fell upon a charm bracelet dangling with hearts, moons, and stars.

"That's pretty."

Ben picked up the bracelet and wrapped it around Lexie's wrist. "Looks nice on you."

"A pretty present for a pretty girl," the vendor commented. She was an elderly woman who wore her snow-white hair in a bun. Hanging around her neck was a pair of glasses on a gold chain.

Lexie blushed.

"Do you like it?" Ben asked.

"I've always wanted a charm bracelet," Lexie admitted.

"How much?"

"Since it's for your girlfriend, I'll give you a discount," the woman said. "Twenty-five dollars."

"I'm not his girlfriend," Lexie said in a rush.

*Why'd she answer so fast?* Ben wondered. *Is there something wrong with being my girlfriend?*

The old woman smiled. "You should be. He seems like a very nice guy."

Now it was Ben's turn to blush.

"You better snatch him up before somebody else does," the old woman continued. She put on her glasses and studied Ben and Lexie. "You both look very nice. Tell you what. I'll still give you the discount."

"Do you like it?" Ben asked Lexie again.

"Yes, but you don't have to buy it for me."

"I want to," Ben insisted. "A reminder of

the day you went to the flea market —"

Lexie cut him off. "But I bought other things."

"— with me," Ben finished.

After bargaining with the vendor, Ben bought the bracelet for fifteen dollars.

Lexie admired the bracelet on her wrist as they continued on their way. "Thanks for the bracelet, Ben. You didn't have to buy it for me."

"I know I didn't. I wanted to."

Lexie wrapped an arm around Ben's and gave it a squeeze before letting go. "You're a really good friend."

Ben cringed hearing those words. Is that all Lexie thought of him as? A friend? He didn't want to be her friend! He wanted to be her boyfriend.

As they passed a booth selling old comic books, Ben stopped.

"Do you collect comics?" Lexie asked.

Ben flipped through a box of comics encased in plastic holders. "My little brother does. I'm always trying to find issues he doesn't have."

"You have a little brother?" Lexie sounded surprised. "I thought you were an only child."

Ben froze. His heart thumped in his chest

and his mouth turned dry. He'd goofed big-time!

"Who told you that?" he casually asked, continuing to flip through the comics.

"Ryan."

Ben did some quick thinking. "My mom got remarried last year. He's actually my stepbrother."

Ben watched Lexie, waiting to see if she believed him. Or had he made matters worse trying to cover up his mistake? He didn't know anything about Ben Holt's family. For all he knew, Ben Holt's mother was dead.

"Your stepbrother's pretty lucky," Lexie said.

Ben abandoned the comics, wanting Lexie to forget about the conversation they'd had. "Want to get some ice cream?"

"Okay."

When they reached the concession stand, Lexie reached into her bag for money. "My treat," she insisted. "What flavor do you want?"

"Chocolate," Ben answered. "It's my favorite."

Lexie's eyes widened. "Mine too."

"I wonder what else we have in common," Ben said.

"Guess we'll have to find out," Lexie said as she handed Ben his cone.

"I guess we will."

They sat at a picnic table eating their ice cream. "I'm all shopped out," Lexie said. "What do you want to do next?"

Ben checked the time on his watch. It was four o'clock. "It's still kind of hot. Want to cool off at the beach?"

Lexie took a lick of her ice cream. "What if we run into Joel? Or Pam and Dionne?"

"We don't have to go to the beach in Southvale. There's a beach between here and Berkley Heights. They've even got a boardwalk and rides."

"Sounds like fun. Let's go!"

They hopped back into the Corvette and drove to the beach. After parking, they walked up to the boardwalk, side by side, Ben's hand brushing against Lexie's. All afternoon at the flea market, Ben had wanted to hold hands with Lexie but thought she wouldn't like it.

Now he decided to take a chance.

He took Lexie's hand in his.

Ben waited to see if Lexie would slip her hand out of his, but she didn't.

She didn't let go.

"The water looks great," Lexie said as

they walked down from the boardwalk to the beach.

"I'll bet it feels great, too."

Suddenly Ben had an idea. A totally spontaneous idea that Lexie was either going to love or hate.

There was only one way to find out.

Ben scooped Lexie up in his arms and ran toward the shore.

"Ben!" Lexie shrieked. "Don't you dare!"

Ben stopped at the edge of the shore. "Don't what?"

"Don't throw me in!"

"Okay, I won't throw you in," he agreed.

Lexie's body sagged with relief.

"I'll throw both of us!" Ben shouted as he ran into the water with Lexie.

Lexie screamed, but her screams were screams of delight. A wave was coming in and Ben threw himself and Lexie directly into it.

The water was cold but refreshing. Ben swam over to Lexie's side as she emerged from underwater.

"Feel better?" Ben asked.

"My bracelet!" Lexie cried, clutching her wrist. "I've lost my charm bracelet."

"Where?"

She pointed to the spot where she'd been swimming. "There."

Ben peered into the water. "I don't see anything."

"Look closer," Lexie begged. "Please."

Ben lowered his head closer to the water.

"Sucker!" Lexie cried gleefully, dunking Ben's head under the water.

When he came back up for air, Lexie was a safe distance away, the charm bracelet on her wrist glistening in the sun. "You're in trouble now," Ben warned playfully, swimming toward Lexie. "This means war!"

After that, they took turns dunking and splashing each other until they were too exhausted to do anything else.

"Today's been great," Lexie said. "It's the most fun I've had in a long time. You're a terrific friend, Ben."

There it was again, Ben thought. That word. *Friend.*

Lexie must have sensed something was bothering him. "What's the matter?" she immediately asked.

They stood on the edge of the water, waves lapping at their feet. Overhead, seagulls screamed in the air.

"I don't want to be your friend," Ben said, scrunching his toes in the wet sand.

"You don't?"

Ben lifted his head. Lexie looked crushed and his heart melted.

"Why not?" she asked.

"I want to be more than a friend."

"What do you want to be?"

"I want to be your boyfriend," Ben whispered.

He didn't give Lexie a chance to answer. Instead, he closed the distance between them, cradling her face between his hands as he pressed his lips softly against hers.

# Chapter 10

It was the perfect kiss.

Ben knew it. It felt right. The rest of the world faded away as Lexie's lips melted against his. She was the only person who existed for him.

Her arms wrapped around him, pulling him closer. Their kiss deepened and then they pulled away from each other.

"Wow," Lexie whispered.

"Wow," Ben echoed.

Lexie stepped away from Ben. She gave him an embarrassed smile and turned her head away, gazing out at the water. "I didn't expect that. I mean, I like you, Ben, but I never thought of you *that way*."

"Why not?" Lexie didn't answer and Ben placed a hand on her shoulder. "Look at me, Lexie."

Lexie turned around. "I don't know," she

answered. "I told you all about Joel. He really hurt me."

"I'm not Joel. I'm not going to hurt you."

"I wasn't looking for a new boyfriend."

"You've found one."

Lexie shook her head. "I don't know if I'm ready."

"Aren't you ever going to fall in love again?"

"I've never been in love. I told you that the other night."

"Then how will you know what it's like to fall in love if you don't take another chance?" Ben argued. "I just might be the guy you've been waiting for."

"Am I the girl you've been waiting for?"

"Yes," Ben confessed.

"Why? What's so special about me?"

"Everything," Ben answered. "I like you, Lexie. I like being with you and spending time together. I guess I've been falling in love with you since the first time we met. Even after your nasty cat scratched me."

Lexie gave Ben a small smile. "I'm afraid," she confessed. "I don't want to be hurt again."

Ben moved closer to Lexie. He wrapped his arms around her waist and looked down at her. Her face, filled with trust and fear and longing, stared up at him.

"Give us a chance, Lexie. I won't hurt you."

"Promise?"

Ben sighed. "I can't promise that, Lexie. I would never intentionally hurt you, but sometimes things happen and we don't have any control over them. Like if a person does something wrong, but it's for a good reason." *Like pretending to be someone they're not,* Ben thought.

Lexie's arms slipped around Ben's neck. "At least you're honest."

"Why don't I help you make up your mind?"

"How?"

Ben kissed Lexie gently on the forehead. Then his lips moved down to her nose and finally to her lips. Ben hesitated before kissing Lexie on the lips again, but all hesitation disappeared when she pressed her lips against his. Ben didn't need any further encouragement, kissing Lexie deeply. Intensely.

Their second kiss was just as wonderful as their first. When it ended, Lexie was smiling at Ben.

"You can be a pretty persuasive guy," she said.

"I try."

Lexie clasped Ben's hand in hers. "We've got the entire summer to spend together," she said. "Why don't we see how it goes? Maybe by the end of August we'll be a couple."

"If that's what you want."

Lexie nodded. "I do, but there's one other thing."

"What?"

"Can I have another kiss?"

Ben promptly did as asked.

They spent the rest of the afternoon walking along the beach, holding hands and collecting seashells as the sun dried their wet clothes. As the sun started to set, they left the beach and walked along the boardwalk. The bright lights and shrieks of delight coming from the many rides were irresistible and soon Ben and Lexie were racing from the Ferris wheel to the roller coaster and bumper cars. After they finished with the rides, they explored the boardwalk some more and spent an hour in the arcades before deciding to get something to eat.

They were munching on messy chili dogs when they passed a sketch artist.

"Hey, here's your chance to do what

you've always wanted," Ben said, wiping his mouth with a napkin.

"What?" Lexie asked.

"Sketch!"

Ben asked the artist, a redhead with glasses who looked like he was in college, if Lexie could sketch his portrait.

"Sure," the guy agreed.

At first Lexie resisted, but Ben finally wore her down.

"I thought this was what you wanted to do when you graduated from college," Ben said.

"Yes, but I'm not as good as he is," Lexie said, glancing at the sketches on display.

"Just do your best. Come on, Lexie. For me, please?"

Lexie sighed and sat down in front of an easel with a blank piece of paper. "If I don't like it when I'm through, I get to rip it into teeny-tiny pieces. Deal?"

Ben sat in the chair in front of Lexie. "Deal."

As Lexie sketched, her nervousness slipped away and she started to get into the mood. Every so often she would order Ben to "Sit still!" or "Don't move!" as she focused more and more on the drawing before her. Finally, she put down her pencil.

"Are you finished?" Ben asked, jumping out of his seat. "Can I see?"

Lexie didn't answer. She studied the easel in front of her and then nodded.

Ben was amazed when he saw the finished sketch. It was terrific. Almost like staring at a photo.

"It's great, Lexie," Ben complimented. "You're really talented."

"You're just saying that," Lexie said.

"No, he isn't," the sketch artist commented. He was standing behind Lexie, looking over her shoulder at the sketch. "You really are good. You could make money doing this."

"It's not that good." Lexie looked at the sketch, then at Ben and the sketch artist. "Is it?"

*Why does she sound so uncertain?* Ben wondered. Anyone with a set of eyes could see Lexie had talent. With the right studying and training, she could become a famous artist. Didn't Lexie's parents encourage her? Or did they *discourage* her because they wanted her to be what they wanted?

The sketch artist, who introduced himself as Sean, started talking with Lexie, pointing out tiny things he would have done differently if he'd sketched Ben's portrait. As he talked, Lexie kept nodding her head. Ben could see she was absorbing everything Sean was saying.

"You want to take over for a little while?" Sean asked. "I haven't eaten all day and I'm starving. I need a break."

"Me?" Lexie gasped, a panicked look on her face. "What do I do?"

Sean laughed. "What you just did with your friend. Sit the customer down and sketch. Any sales you make are yours."

After Sean left, Lexie admitted to Ben, "I hope no one asks me to sketch them."

"Why?"

"I'm too nervous. I'll mess up."

"You will not."

Lexie giggled. "My parents would freak out if they knew I was taking money from strangers."

"It's not taking money from strangers. You're doing a job and they're paying you for it."

"I've never had a job before."

"Really?"

"It's not that I haven't wanted to," Lexie explained. "I'd love to make some money of my own instead of always having to ask my dad. I'd feel more independent, you know?"

"So why don't you?"

Lexie sighed. "He won't let me. It's as if it's beneath me and my sisters to work. Not that they want to until they have to. And then it'll be for big bucks and not minimum wage. I'm the only odd one."

*He'd flip his lid if he knew you were dating a maid,* Ben thought.

"Why do you think he feels that way?" Ben asked.

"I told you. My parents are snobs. All they care about is appearances. It's like they're petrified someone at their country club will see me working at the mall and hold it against them."

Just then a couple asked Lexie to sketch them together. She was nervous at first, but as she became more involved with her sketching, the nervousness soon disappeared. She was finishing up when Sean returned.

"Nice job," Sean complimented.

The couple was equally thrilled and happily paid Lexie for their sketch. After they left, Lexie stared at the ten dollars in her hand with disbelief.

"I can't believe they paid me to sketch them," she whispered. "I made money from sketching!"

Sean sat back down in front of his easel. "Keep at it and you'll make a lot more."

"Come on," Lexie urged Ben. "Let's go buy some dessert." She waved the ten-dollar bill in her hand. "My treat!"

They bought sticks of blue cotton candy and ate them on their way back to Ben's car. Lexie rested her head on Ben's shoulder as they walked, still excited about her first sale.

"I can really do it if I want to," Lexie exclaimed. "If I want to sell sketches, I can. I'm good at it."

"Didn't anyone ever tell you that?"

Lexie shook her head.

"Not even your parents?"

"No," Lexie whispered. "I told you. They want me to have a high-powered job. A career. They think my sketches are fine, but they don't encourage my interest in art."

"They're wrong, Lexie. Don't ever forget that. If you want to be an artist, you can."

Lexie nodded her head, gazing at the sketch she'd done of Ben. "I know."

"I get to keep that, right?" he asked.

Lexie held the sketch out of Ben's grasp. "After you buy it from me."

"Will I be able to afford it?"

Lexie smiled at Ben. "Oh, I think you'll be able to afford this."

"How much?"

"One kiss."

Ben pretended to think for a second. "Seems reasonable."

Taking Lexie in his arms, Ben gave her a kiss. It was a soft, gentle kiss and as their lips met he could taste cotton candy on her lips. It made their kiss sweet and delicious.

"Sold," Lexie whispered, handing the sketch to Ben before slipping into the front seat of the car.

It was a warm night, so they drove with the top down on the convertible. When they returned to the club, Ben's plan was to walk Lexie to her door and kiss her good night. Then he'd head to Ben Holt's bungalow, stay out of sight for a couple of minutes, and drive back home.

But Lexie changed all that in the club's parking lot.

"I'm going to go to my bungalow and take a shower," she said. "You probably want to do the same. Why don't you knock on my door in thirty minutes?"

Ben sneaked a peek at his watch. It was already nine o'clock. If he spent an hour with Lexie, it'd be ten-thirty when he left the club for his hour-long drive. He was cutting it close, but he still had time to get home before his midnight curfew.

Ben took a shower in Benjamin Holt's bungalow. He didn't want to wear any of Ben Holt's clothes again — who knew how much they cost — but how would he explain showing up in the same outfit? He searched through Ben's closet for a pair of shorts and a T-shirt. He finally found a pair of khaki shorts and a plaid shirt that didn't look like they'd cost too much to replace if something happened to them. Just to make sure, he double-checked inside for designer labels but didn't find any.

After combing his hair, Ben headed next door to Lexie's. He knocked on her door once, then twice. On the other side, he heard approaching footsteps. The door opened and Ben expected to see Lexie.

It was Dionne.

"Hi," he said. Ben gave Dionne a friendly smile, deciding he'd try to be nice to her. "What are you doing here?"

"Hanging out."

Ben followed Dionne into the living room, where Pam was lying across the sofa, watching music videos on TV. Astrid was perched at her feet. At the sight of Ben she hissed and then ran off into the bedroom.

"We were telling Lexie all about Joel's pool party," Dionne said, sitting cross-legged on the floor.

"It was a blast," Pam commented.

Lexie came out of the bedroom, brushing her hair. She'd changed into white jeans and a blue blouse. The colors highlighted her tan.

"We had a fun day, too," Lexie said, sitting next to Ben on a flowered love seat. She held out her wrist. "Ben bought me this charm bracelet."

Pam and Dionne glanced at the bracelet. "Nice," Pam said.

"So what do you want to do?" Dionne asked. "We've been waiting forever for you to get back."

"Want to catch a movie?" Lexie asked. "We could go to the drive-in."

"If you don't have a boyfriend or a date, a drive-in isn't any fun," Dionne stated. "Thumbs-down."

"Why don't we invite some people over?" Pam suggested.

"Like who?" Lexie asked suspiciously.

"Not Joel," Pam said, sitting up. "He's at home. But Holly, Dane, Julie, and Noah are hanging out by the pool."

"A party sounds like fun," Lexie agreed.

"Great!" Pam exclaimed. "I'll go get them."

Fifteen minutes later there was a party in Lexie's bungalow. Music was blasting from the CD player and Dionne had called room service for lots of munchies and sodas. There were also more guests than those Pam had invited. Word about the party had spread and friends of friends kept showing up.

Ben stayed for as long as he could, listening to music and dancing with Lexie, but finally he had to leave. When it came to curfew, his dad was strict.

"Are you sure you can't stay?" Lexie asked, walking Ben outside. "You've only been here for an hour."

"You know I don't want to leave," Ben explained. "But I'm really tired. I can't keep my eyes open another second."

Lexie walked Ben to his bungalow door. "Well, get a good night's sleep." She gave Ben a good-night kiss on the cheek. "I'll see you tomorrow."

Ben watched as Lexie walked back to her bungalow. At the door, she turned around and waved. Ben waved back as he stepped into his bungalow and closed the door.

Inside the bungalow, Ben turned on the TV and settled on the couch. He'd stay inside for a couple of minutes until he was sure the coast was clear outside and then head for the parking lot.

Watching TV, Ben's eyelids began to grow heavy. He really was tired. Maybe he'd rest his eyes for a minute.

The next time Ben opened his eyes, there was fuzz on the TV screen. At first he didn't know where he was. Nothing looked familiar. This wasn't his bedroom. Where was he?

As his eyes adjusted to the darkness, he recognized pieces of furniture. He was in Ben Holt's bungalow. But what was he doing here? Why wasn't he home in his own bed? What time was it?

Ben turned on a light next to the couch and checked the time on his watch. He nearly choked. Two o'clock in the morning! He should have been home two hours ago. His father was going to ground him for life.

Ben scrambled to his feet. He shut off the TV and hurried out of the bungalow.

Outside, the ground was wet and the trees were heavy with raindrops. It must have stormed while he was sleeping. Ben didn't give the rain much thought until he reached the parking lot.

And then he remembered.

He'd forgotten to put the top back up on the convertible.

Ben dragged his feet to the car.

When he looked inside, it was just as bad as he thought it would be.

The whole inside of the car was soaked.

Ray was going to kill him. How could he have forgotten to put the top back up? He'd promised Ray he would be extra careful with his father's car and he'd let him down.

Ben slipped behind the steering wheel, sitting in a puddle of water. He couldn't worry about the car now. He'd take care of it tomorrow morning. Right now, he had to get home.

Even though the roads were deserted and his foot was itching to press down on the gas, Ben made sure he didn't go above the speed limit. The last thing he wanted was a ticket. Or an accident.

When he pulled into his driveway, he knew he was in big trouble. All the lights were on in the house.

His father was waiting at the front door, wearing a robe over his pajamas. Before Ben could even say anything, his father was roaring.

"Where have you been, young man? It's

three o'clock in the morning. Your mother and I have been out of our minds with worry!"

"I —" Ben started to say, but his dad cut him off.

"We thought something had happened to you. We thought you might have been in an accident. We've been calling all your friends and no one knew where you were."

In the living room, Ben could see his mom sitting on the sofa. She hadn't even changed for bed. He knew she always waited up till he got home. The last three hours must have been awful for her. He felt even worse.

"I'm sorry," Ben said. "I was at the club. There was a party and I fell asleep watching TV."

"You know you have a curfew."

"I know," Ben said.

"Why didn't you call us when you woke up?"

"I didn't think of it. I'm sorry."

"Sorry isn't enough." Mr. Harris sighed and ran a hand through his hair. It was black with streaks of gray mixed in. Ben figured he'd probably added a bunch more gray tonight.

"We'll deal with this in the morning."

Ben's mother joined his father's side. "Ray's been calling all night," she said.

"I'll call him in the morning."

"Where did you get those clothes?" Mrs. Harris asked. "I've never seen them before."

"From a friend," Ben said, forcing out the words. He hated lying to his mother.

"Whose car is that in the driveway?" Mr. Harris asked.

"Ray lent me his father's convertible. I had a date and I wanted to impress her."

As soon as the words were out of his mouth, Ben knew he had made a mistake. A *big* one. "*Ray* lent you his *father's* convertible? Does Mr. Preston know about this?"

Ben squirmed, knowing he'd just gotten Ray into hot water. "I don't think so."

"Why not?"

"Mr. Preston is out of town."

Ben's father pointed to the stairs. "To bed. We'll discuss *all* of this in the morning."

Ben didn't like the sound of that. He opened his mouth to protest, but after one look at his father he closed his mouth and trudged upstairs to his room.

# Chapter 11

Ben's parents laid down the law at breakfast the following morning. He was grounded. For the next two weeks he was to come straight home from work. No movies. No beach. No parties. No dates.

Ben thought his punishment too strict and tried to get his dad to agree to a compromise. After all, it wasn't like he had stayed out late on purpose.

His dad wouldn't listen to any of his arguments. "This isn't just about staying out late last night," Mr. Harris lectured, glowering at Ben over his newspaper. "It's also about borrowing Mr. Preston's convertible. You had no right driving his car. Not to mention the fact that you've ruined the interior with your carelessness."

After those words, Ben slumped down in his seat, picking at his oatmeal until his dad went to work outside. Once he was gone, Ben tried pleading with his mother, but she was just as stern.

"You have to learn responsibility, Ben. Maybe the next time you borrow something that doesn't belong to you, you'll be more careful."

"Yeah," Dougie chimed in, pouring orange juice over his Froot Loops.

Ben threw a small piece of toast at Dougie, who wailed when it hit his arm. "Mom!"

Mrs. Harris sighed and turned from the sink where she was washing dishes. "Ben, do you want to be grounded for three weeks?" She pointed a finger at Dougie, who was smiling smugly at Ben. "And if you bother your brother one more time today, mister, you'll be grounded, too."

Dougie's smug smile disappeared.

"Aren't you late for work?" Mrs. Harris asked, glancing at the clock over the stove.

"It's my day off," Ben said. He'd been planning to drive over to the club after lunch, but since he was grounded that wasn't going to happen. Two whole weeks without seeing Lexie. He didn't know how he would stand it. He'd have to come up with some way to see her at the club while he was working. But what was he going to tell her when she wanted to see him at night?

"Is it okay if I swing by Ray's job to tell him what happened to his father's car?" Ben asked. "I'd rather do it in person than over the phone."

"As long as you come right back when you're finished," Mrs. Harris reminded him. "Since you're going to be around the house for the next two weeks, I've got a whole list of chores for you to do. You can start by cleaning out the attic and basement."

"Don't worry, Ben," Dougie added, munching on his cereal. "I'll hang out with you when you're not working."

Ben sighed as he left the kitchen. It was going to be a long two weeks.

When Ben showed up at Dog Gone Clean, Ray was in the middle of washing a poodle in a tub of sudsy water. At the sight of Ben, Ray abandoned the drenched dog to a coworker. He wiped his wet hands on a towel as he rushed over to Ben.

"Where's my dad's car? What happened to it? What did you do?"

Ray shot his questions one after another

at Ben, not giving him a chance to answer. Ray glanced out the front window of Dog Gone Clean into the street. "Why isn't my dad's car parked by the curb? Why is your Dodge there?"

"Ray, your dad's car is fine."

"Then why isn't it out there?" Ray demanded, his voice rising. "Where is it? Don't jerk me around, Ben. Something's up. I can tell. You're not looking me in the eye. You always do that when something's wrong."

"It's not as bad as it sounds," Ben mumbled, staring at the floor.

"Oh, no!" Ray wailed. "When someone says something like that, it *is* bad!"

"Well," Ben admitted, lifting his head, "there's a problem."

"A problem?" Ray's voice squeaked.

"A small one," Ben rushed to say.

"What happened? Did you dent the car?"

"No."

"Hit a tree? Scratch the paint? Bump a fender?"

"No, no, no," Ben answered.

"Then what?" Ray demanded.

"I forgot to put the top up last night."

Ray's mouth dropped open. "You forgot

. . . to put . . . the top up," he whispered hoarsely. "It rained last night, Ben. It poured!"

"I know," Ben said in a small voice. "But don't worry, Ray. My dad took the car in to a car wash this morning. I'm going to pay to have all the upholstery dry-cleaned. And if it can't be repaired, then I'll pay to have it replaced."

"You know what this means?" Ray moaned. "My dad's going to find out I lent you his car."

"I'm sorry, Ray."

"He's going to go ballistic and ground me forever. Or at least for the rest of the summer. Why didn't you remember to put the top up?"

"Lexie caught me off guard last night."

"What does she have to do with this?"

"After we left the beach, we drove back to the club with the top down. I thought I was going to come straight home after dropping her off, but I didn't. When I parked the car, I forgot to put the top up."

"So it's because of your girlfriend that I'm going to be in hot water with my father?"

"Don't blame Lexie," Ben said. "Even if I'd remembered to put the top up, we'd still be in trouble."

"What are you talking about?"

"My dad knows you lent me your father's car without asking permission," Ben admitted.

"How does he know that?"

"I told him."

"You *told* him?" Ray shouted. "What are you? Crazy?"

"Don't get mad, Ray," Ben pleaded. "Let me tell you what happened last night."

Ray folded his arms over his chest and leaned against a wall. "This better be good."

Ben told Ray the whole story. When he finished, Ray was shaking his head.

"Ben, this is getting out of control. Look at what's happened. You've gotten grounded, I'm going to get grounded, and you're going to have to take more money out of the bank to fix my dad's car. Since taking this summer job you've been *losing* money instead of *making* money. No girl is worth all this trouble."

"Lexie is."

"She likes you," Ray said. "Don't you think you should tell her the truth?"

"I will, but not yet."

"When?"

"At the end of the summer."

"The only reason you're going to tell her

then is because you'll have to," Ray stated. "You won't have a spare bungalow and you won't be able to fool her into thinking you're rich."

Ben shook his head. "That's not true. I can't tell her the truth now because I don't think she would forgive me," he admitted. "She likes me, but she doesn't care enough about me. She wouldn't give me a second chance. And I'm afraid."

"Of what?"

"Her old boyfriend wants her back. If I tell Lexie the truth, she might get back together with him."

"I thought you said she couldn't stand him."

"She can't. But if I really hurt her, he'd use that to his advantage."

"You're making a mess out of your life, Ben. You know that, don't you?"

"I know," Ben admitted. "I know. But how much worse can it get?"

# Chapter 12

Things got much worse the following day.

Ben's day started the way it usually did. He arrived at work at nine o'clock, went down to housekeeping, loaded his cart with fresh towels, sheets, cleaning supplies, and paper products, and started his rounds at ten.

An hour later Ben was pushing his cart down a hallway, getting ready to clean a new row of rooms, when he heard voices. At first he didn't pay attention to them. Lots of times there were guests in the hallways, heading out to the beach or coming back to their rooms for something they'd forgotten.

But as the voices drew nearer, Ben stopped what he was doing.

The voices he heard sounded familiar.

*Very* familiar.

He listened more closely.

As he did, he recognized the voices and his heart nearly stopped.

It was Pam, Dionne, and Lexie.

And they were headed his way!

Ben dropped the towels in his arms and looked around in panic, trying to find a place to hide. They couldn't see him like this! Not the way he was dressed. He was wearing his smock that had SOUTHVALE SWIM AND SUN CLUB etched on the back. On the front there was a patch over his heart that said HOUSEKEEPING.

Ben tried to find some way to escape, but there was nowhere to go. There were no stairs to run down and the hallway ended at a wall.

He was trapped. In a second Lexie was going to come around the corner and see him.

Ben's mind scrambled for some way to get himself out of this mess. He couldn't lose Lexie. Not now. Not when they were just starting to get to know each other.

Suddenly he had an idea.

Ben knocked frantically on a door and called out, "Housekeeping." When there was no answer, he used his master key and slipped into the room.

His body sagged with relief as he rested against the closed door.

He'd stay behind the door until they were gone.

Outside, he could hear approaching footsteps, as well as the sound of voices getting closer.

And closer.

Ben expected to hear the footsteps and voices fading away.

But they didn't.

The footsteps stopped outside the room.

Then he heard a key inserted in the lock.

Ben's blood turned cold at the sound. He began backing away from the door in horror as the doorknob started to turn and the door began opening.

He had to hide.

Ben ran to the closet, jumping inside and closing the door behind him in the nick of time.

"I can't believe I forgot my wallet," Dionne said, finding it on top of a dresser. She slipped it into her canvas tote bag. "Ready to hit the beach?"

Inside the closet, Ben gave a sigh of relief. They were leaving.

"What's your rush? Those hunky lifeguards don't come on duty for another half hour," Pam said. She aimed the remote control at the TV. "Let's veg out for a bit and watch some game shows."

Hearing those words, Ben groaned. It was starting to get hot inside the closet and he was sweating. Plus, what if Dionne wanted something from the closet? What was he going to say when she opened the door?

"It's too nice out to stay inside," Lexie said, checking her hair in the dresser mirror. "I want to go down to the beach."

"And find your beach boy?" Dionne teased.

"Who?" Lexie asked.

"You know who. That guy you're madly in love with. Ben."

"I'm not madly in love with Ben," Lexie said. "But I do like him. A lot."

Ben smiled when he heard Lexie's words. She liked him! He pressed his ear closer to the closet door, wanting to hear more.

"So where is lover boy?" Pam asked. "I haven't seen him around."

"I don't know," Lexie answered. "I didn't see him at all yesterday. I've been calling his bungalow and there's no answer. I even slipped a note under his door. I hope he's okay."

"Why are you so crazy about him?" Dionne asked. "He's not like any of the guys we hang out with."

"That's right," Lexie said. "He's not a jock or a muscle-head or a preppy. He's different. He's sweet and funny and when we're together, he makes me feel like I'm the only person who exists. I never felt that way with Joel or any of the other guys I dated. They were only dating me because I was pretty and popular. I don't want to be treated like an accessory. I want to be liked for who I am."

"I guess he must like you if he bought you that bracelet," Dionne grudgingly admitted. "Where'd he get it? Antonio's at the mall?"

"No." Lexie twirled the bracelet around her wrist. "At a flea market."

"A flea market?" Pam gasped. "You've got to be kidding!"

"What's wrong with that?" Lexie asked. "It's pretty and I love it."

"How cheap can you get!" Dionne exclaimed. "Has your wrist turned green yet?"

"Joel would buy you a *real* bracelet," Pam stated. "Made of gold. He'd buy you anything you wanted."

"I don't want a bracelet from Joel," Lexie

said. "And I don't want anything else from him. I wish he'd leave me alone."

"Why don't you give him a second chance, Lexie?" Dionne asked. "He really wants to get back together with you."

Lexie's voice turned hard. "I don't want to give him a second chance. How can you even ask me to do that? You know the way he hurt me. He broke up with me a week before the Junior Prom and went with some-one else."

"He's sorry," Dionne said.

"Sorry's not good enough," Lexie said. "It's over. I'm dating Ben. He makes me feel spe-cial and he'd never hurt me the way Joel did."

Listening in the closet, Ben suddenly felt guilty for lying to Lexie. He knew she would be hurt if she found out the truth. After all, he wasn't being honest with her. And if she thought he was a liar, she wouldn't believe anything he told her. Including the way he felt about her.

"I don't want to talk about Joel anymore," Lexie stated, walking to the door. "I'm going down to the beach. Maybe Ben's there. I'll see you guys later."

"We've got to talk to Joel," Dionne said af-ter Lexie left. "This is more serious than we thought."

"What do you think she sees in that guy?" Pam asked.

"He's being nice to her and she's falling for it because she's on the rebound from Joel. That's all."

"You think?"

"I'm positive. But there's something else going on. Have you noticed the way he's uncomfortable around us?"

"That's because he knows we don't like him."

Dionne shook her head. "No, it's more than that. He never wants to talk about himself and he avoids answering questions. He's hiding something. But what?"

Pam shrugged. "I don't know."

"We're going to find out," Dionne insisted. "And we'll get Joel to help us."

Uh-oh. Ben didn't like Dionne's words. If he wanted to avoid trouble, he'd have to steer clear of her and Pam and Joel.

"Are you sure we should be doing this?" Pam asked. "Lexie might get mad."

"Lexie isn't thinking straight. She and Joel belong together. You know how stubborn she can be when her feelings are hurt. She won't even give Joel a second chance and that's not like her!"

"He did dump her the week before the Junior Prom," Pam pointed out. "That was pretty low."

"It's not like he stood her up the night of the prom," Dionne argued. "Lexie could have gotten another date. Plenty of guys wanted to go with her, but she turned them all down."

"I guess." Pam turned off the TV. "Let's go to the beach. The life-hunks are probably there by now."

"Just let me get my beach jacket," Dionne said, heading for the closet.

Inside the closet, Ben heard Dionne's approaching footsteps with dread.

The closet door started to open.

Ben pressed himself into the farthest corner of the closet, pulling himself into a ball. It was dark in the closet. Maybe she wouldn't notice him. Maybe she'd only stick a hand inside and reach for the hanger with her beach jacket.

The door opened a bit wider. Light began to filter inside the closet, falling over Ben's sneakers.

Ben squeezed his eyes shut, wishing he could become invisible. This was it. It was all over. He was going to be exposed.

He waited for Dionne's shriek of outrage.

But it didn't come. Instead, he heard Pam's voice.

"You left your beach jacket in my cabana yesterday. Don't you remember?"

"That's right," Dionne slammed the closet door shut. "Let's go."

Ben listened to Dionne and Pam leave the room. He wiped away a sheen of sweat from his forehead.

"Phew," he whispered. "That was close."

# Chapter 13

Ben hid in the closet for an extra ten minutes, wanting to make sure Dionne and Pam didn't come back for anything else they might have forgotten. When he felt it was safe, he slipped out of the closet and slowly opened the door to the room. He stuck his head out into the hallway cautiously, looking to the left and right, making sure the coast was clear before dashing to his cleaning cart.

But as Ben started pushing his cart down the hallway, he heard approaching footsteps. He instantly stopped, trying to hear voices, but all was silent. Except for the footsteps drawing closer. Could it be Pam or Dionne returning? Even worse, could it be Lexie?

Ben chewed on his lower lip. There wasn't time to rush back into Dionne's room. And he couldn't sneak into another room without knocking and announcing himself. If he called out and it was Pam, Dionne, or Lexie coming his way, they'd hear him. And they'd want to know why he was calling out, "Housekeeping."

Ben stared at his cleaning cart, wishing he could hide behind it. It was big enough, but there was still the chance of being noticed.

Unless he hid *inside* the cart.

Without wasting another second, Ben threw himself into the deep cart, pulling piles of sheets and dirty towels over himself.

He was practically invisible.

All he'd have to do now is wait until the sound of the footsteps disappeared. Then he'd jump out of the cart and be on his way.

The footsteps drew closer and Ben couldn't resist peeking over the edge of the cleaning cart. When he did, he groaned. The footsteps belonged to a young mother who was pushing a baby stroller. He'd overreacted!

Ben started to climb out of the cart, but before he could get a leg out, something unexpected happened.

The cart started to move.

Ben tried to jump out, but the cart was going too fast, picking up speed. Ben gripped the sides of the cart, trying to figure out what to do. Should he try to jump? But what if he sprained his ankle? Or worse, broke his leg?

Before Ben could make up his mind, the cart reached the end of the hallway, crashing into the mouth of the chute that led down to the laundry room. The cart tipped over and Ben slid down the chute, landing in a pile of dirty laundry.

At the other end of the laundry room, one of the maids who worked on Ben's floor was staring at him, her mouth hanging open in surprise.

"Thought I'd take a shortcut," Ben explained before hurrying out of the laundry room and heading back upstairs.

Ben cleaned the rest of his rooms in record time. All he wanted was to put away his cleaning supplies, change out of his uniform, and find Lexie. He'd reached a decision while listening to her words when he was hidden. He had to tell her the truth. Today. He couldn't keep pretending to be something he wasn't. It wasn't right. He only hoped she'd understand why he had lied to her.

Ben Holt's bungalow was the last one Ben had to clean. When he opened the door he found Lexie's note on the floor and eagerly opened it up. It was a short note, with Lexie hoping everything was fine and asking him to call her when he had a chance.

Ben went in search of Lexie after he had finished cleaning the bungalow and changed. He found her on the beach, lying on a towel with her eyes closed, listening to her Walkman. Just then Lexie opened her eyes, shading them from the sun with a hand. When she saw Ben, a big smile spread across her face. Lexie's smile and her delight at seeing him gave Ben a warm feeling inside.

*She likes me. She's happy to see me. When we're not together, she misses me.*

Lexie turned off her Walkman, removing her headphones. "I thought you fell off the face of the earth! Where've you been? I've been calling and calling your bungalow, but there was no answer. Did you get my note?"

Ben held it up. "I had to go out of town with my parents to visit my grandmother. It was her birthday." *Great, I'm telling another lie when I decided I was going to be honest and tell her the truth.*

"I'm glad you're back."

"Me too." Ben took a deep breath. "Lexie, there's something I have to tell you."

"What?" Lexie asked while rummaging through her tote bag.

"Could you look at me?"

Lexie abandoned her tote bag. "What is it, Ben? You look so serious!"

Ben opened his mouth, but the words wouldn't come out. They were sticking in his throat and he couldn't swallow. He hadn't thought it would be this hard.

Lexie got to her feet and placed a hand on Ben's arm. "Ben? What is it?" she asked, her voice filled with concern. "What do you want to tell me?"

"Can we be in on it, too?" Dionne asked, hearing the last of Lexie's words as she and Pam walked up to Lexie's towel. "Or is it a big secret?"

Ben gazed at Dionne and Pam with dismay. He couldn't do it. He couldn't tell Lexie the truth. Not now. Not in front of them. It would be too humiliating. They'd be sure to gloat and would keep Lexie mad at him, doing whatever they could to make sure she wouldn't give him a second chance.

"I missed you," he whispered.

"Is that all?" Lexie exclaimed, relief flooding her face. "You had me worried for a second!"

"What a letdown," Pam said. "We thought you were going to reveal something juicy!"

Ben pulled Lexie off to one side. "Want to get something to eat?" he asked. Maybe he could work up his courage again and tell Lexie the truth over lunch. "Alone."

"We get the hint," Dionne said, eaves-dropping.

"Sure, but can we meet in an hour?" Lexie glanced at the time on her watch. "My parents are supposed to be calling me from Hawaii and I don't want to miss them. Why don't we meet in the club's dining room?"

Ben would have preferred grabbing a burger at the Burger Hut down the beach; the club's prices were sky high. But he couldn't tell that to Lexie. Not while she still thought he was Ben Holt. Luckily, today was payday. While Lexie was on the phone with her parents he'd stop by Gladys's office and pick up his paycheck.

"Okay." Ben wanted to give Lexie a kiss good-bye but felt awkward with Dionne and Pam watching. "I'll see you later."

"Just the guy I'm looking for," Gladys announced, putting down her pen when Ben walked into her office.

"How come?" Ben asked.

"The dining room is short-staffed today. A couple of waiters called in sick and I need as many extra hands as I can get."

"What does that have to do with me?" Ben asked, not liking the way Gladys was staring at him.

"You've got two hands. You're going to use them carrying trays in and out of the kitchen."

"Did you say the *dining* room?" Ben asked.

"Are you hard of hearing?"

"I can't do it," Ben said.

"I think you're misunderstanding me," Gladys said. "I'm not *asking* you to work in the dining room. I'm *telling* you."

"B-B-But I can't," Ben sputtered. He was supposed to meet Lexie in the dining room in an hour, sitting across from her with a menu, not standing above her with an order pad! "I just can't!"

"Why not?"

He couldn't tell Gladys the truth. If he did, he might get fired. After all, he was impersonating a guest *and* using his bungalow. His mind scrambled for an excuse. "I don't know how to be a waiter."

Gladys waved a hand at Ben. "It's easy. All you do is write down the orders, drop them off in the kitchen, and then pick them up when they're done. Mario will show you the ropes." Gladys returned to the papers on her desk, expecting Ben to leave. But he didn't. She stared up at him. "What are you still doing here?"

"I can't be a waiter, Gladys," Ben said, deciding to use the truth as an excuse. "My parents grounded me and I'm supposed to come straight home after I'm finished cleaning rooms."

Gladys pushed her phone toward Ben. "Call them up. I'll explain. They'll make an exception for today."

Ben shook his head. "They won't budge. They're pretty strict."

"Then you're fired," Gladys stated.

"You can't fire me!" Ben exclaimed.

"Yes, I can," Gladys answered. "I'm your boss and when I tell you to do something, you do it. Everyone at the Southvale Swim and Sun Club works together as a team. If you can't be a team player, then I don't want you on my staff."

"But that's not fair," Ben protested.

Gladys shrugged. "Who said life was fair? Those are the rules. *My* rules. Either you follow them or you don't. If you don't, you can find yourself another job."

Ben knew when he was licked. Gladys was calling the shots. He didn't want to lose his job, but what was he going to tell Lexie when she saw him waiting on tables? Ben picked up the phone and dialed his house, handing the receiver to Gladys. "Fine," he grumbled. "I'll do it."

"Why are you making such a big deal out of this?" Gladys asked, cradling the receiver against her ear. "It's only for one afternoon and you'll be paid extra for your time. What's wrong with that? I thought you liked money."

*Not as much as I like Lexie,* Ben thought. He stared glumly at the clock over Gladys's desk as time ticked away. He felt like he had a noose around his neck and it was growing tighter and tighter with each passing second. Unless he figured out something fast, his romance with Lexie would be over within an hour.

# Chapter 14

After leaving Gladys's office, Ben raced to the nearest pay phone and made a second call. He had come up with an idea, but he needed Ray's help. He couldn't do it without him.

Ben crossed his fingers as the phone rang, hoping Ray would answer. He had to. He was his only hope. After the fifth ring, Ray picked up. Ben didn't give him a chance to say anything else after hello, rushing to get out his words.

"Ray, I need your help."

There was silence on the other end of the line, followed by a sigh. "Don't you have any other friends?"

"I don't have time for jokes. This is serious."

"What happened now?" Ray asked. "Wait! Don't answer. Let me use my ESP powers and guess. It involves Lexie."

"My boss wants me to work in the dining room as a waiter at lunch because we're short-staffed."

"What's wrong with that?"

"I'm supposed to have lunch with Lexie in the dining room!"

"Uh-oh," Ray murmured. "Trouble."

"Big-time."

"Can't you get out of waitering?"

"I tried. Gladys told me if I don't do it, I'm fired."

"Then cancel your lunch date with Lexie," Ray said. "Simple enough."

"That still doesn't solve my problem. What if Pam and Dionne are in the dining room? Or Joel? If they see me, my goose is cooked."

"Charbroiled is more like it," Ray stated. "So what do you want me to do?"

"Get over here as fast as you can with your makeup kit. The one you used last Halloween at your costume party."

"What do you want it for?"

"Your kit has lots of good disguises. I want to change the way I look. Bring it to Ben Holt's bungalow." Ben glanced at his watch. "And get here as fast as you can, Ray. Every second counts!"

\* \* \*

"What do you mean, this is all you could come up with?" Ben stared at the long curly red wig, press-on nails, and cosmetics that Ray had brought. "I'm not going to dress up like a girl!"

"I'm sorry, Ben, but my cousin Mike borrowed my makeup kit last week for a masquerade party and he didn't return it. I remembered when I went to look for it. This is all I could scrape together on such short notice."

"But I don't want to be a girl!" Ben wailed.

"Why not? It's foolproof!"

"It is?" Ben asked uncertainly.

"If we changed your appearance as a guy, there'd still be a chance that they'd be able to recognize you," Ray explained. "But if you're disguised as a *girl,* they won't suspect a thing."

"Are you sure?"

"Trust me," Ray said. "We'll be able to fool them." He forced Ben into a chair. "Now sit down and shut up." He stared at Ben's face. "Let's see how much I can do without resorting to plastic surgery."

Fifteen minutes later, Ray stepped away from Ben. "Well, you're no supermodel," he commented. "And you're not going to win any beauty contests. But at least you don't look like Ben Harris."

Ben stared at his image in the mirror Ray had been blocking.

A stranger stared back at him.

He wasn't *gorgeous,* but like Ray said, he didn't look like himself.

He looked like a girl — a somewhat *ugly* girl — and not a guy.

In addition to the long curly red wig, Ray had added a pair of cat-eye glasses and penciled some freckles on his nose. There was blush on his cheeks, mascara on his eyelashes, and green eyeshadow on his eyelids. His lips were painted red with lipstick and made shiny with lip gloss.

He'd changed into a waitress uniform with long sleeves that Ashley had dropped off and Ray had stuffed a pair of rolled up tube socks down the front of his chest. "Good thing you don't have hairy legs," Ray said as he added a bunch of bangle bracelets to Ben's wrist.

Ben chewed his lower lip. "Do you think this will work?"

"It better, otherwise you're going to have to explain to Lexie why you're dressed up as a girl. By the way, what are you going to tell

Lexie about not showing up for lunch?"

"I'm going to tell her I fell asleep on the beach."

"Liar, liar, pants on fire," Ray chanted. "Are you sure your name isn't Pinocchio? I think your nose is starting to grow."

At that moment an announcement was made over the club's loudspeaker. "The dining room is now open for lunch."

"I think that's your cue," Ray remarked.

Ben studied himself one last time from head to toe. Then he took a deep breath and headed to the dining room.

The dining room was empty when Ben arrived. Mario had told him which eight tables he'd have to cover, so he headed over to them and busied himself with folding napkins and filling water glasses. Soon guests began strolling in, seating themselves. Some wandered over Ben's way and sat down at his tables.

Handing out menus, Ben introduced himself as Penny, making sure his voice sounded high and feminine. None of the guests gave him a second glance, too busy trying to decide what they wanted for lunch.

Ben kept an eye on the dining room entrance, searching for Lexie, but didn't see her. He felt awful standing her up, but he'd had no choice.

After taking his lunch orders (which was no easy task — it was almost impossible to hold a pen and write with the long nails he was wearing), Ben dropped them off in the kitchen. When they were ready, the chef rang a bell and Ben picked them up. As time flew by, he started to feel better. So far, so good. Maybe he was going to be able to pull this off without a hitch.

Then disaster struck.

Joel showed up with four of his buddies.

And they sat down at one of Ben's tables.

At first Ben thought he could get someone else to take their order. He didn't want to risk Joel recognizing him. But as he glanced around the dining room, he could see all the other waiters and waitresses were busy.

"What do we have to do to get some service around here?" Joel demanded in a bossy voice. He pounded his fist down on the table. Some of the older diners stared in Joel's direction with frowns on their faces, but Joel ignored them, clanging on the side of his water glass with a fork. "Food! Food! Food!" His buddies started doing the same thing.

Afraid that someone might call Mario, Ben snatched up a stack of menus and tucked them under his arm. He approached Joel's table on shaky legs as butterflies swarmed around in his stomach.

*I can get through this,* Ben told himself. *I can fool them. I've fooled everyone else so far. I can fool them. After all, they're not going to pay much attention to me. I'm not the type of girl they'd be interested in.*

"Hi, I'm Penny," he said, handing out menus. His voice sounded shaky and he forced himself to stay calm. "I'll be your waitress."

None of the guys even glanced at Ben twice. They accepted the menus he offered and started reading them. "I'll give you a couple of minutes and then I'll be back to take your orders."

As Ben walked away, he could hear them start to laugh. It was cruel, vicious laughter.

And it was aimed at him.

"Bow-wow! Talk about ugly! Did she escape from the city pound?"

"Anyone got any dog biscuits?"

"Hey, honey, where'd you get the Halloween mask?"

*What a bunch of mean jerks,* Ben thought. How could they be so insensitive to someone else's feelings? Did they think he couldn't hear them? Or did they *want* him to hear?

"Hey, Joel," one of his friends said, "what's the deal with Madison Avenue? She take you back yet or is she too busy spending her daddy's money?"

Everyone at the table laughed.

Madison Avenue? Ben's ears pricked up. That had to be Lexie. He moved closer to the table, wanting to hear more.

"She's still playing hard to get," Joel answered. "It's starting to annoy me. She's so stuck-up."

"Why don't you go after someone else?" another voice asked.

"Why should I? Every guy I know wants to date Madison Avenue. She's got everything. Your social life is guaranteed if you're dating her. She gets invited to all the best parties."

"You never should have dumped her."

"I know. But don't worry. By the end of the summer we'll be a couple again," Joel bragged. "All I have to do is keep saying I'm sorry and she'll believe me. She's such a dummy."

Ben hated hearing Joel's horrible nickname for Lexie and the way he was talking about her. It was time to teach him a lesson.

Ben pasted a sweet smile on his face and moved closer to the table, but not too close. He didn't want them to get too good a look at his face. "Is everyone ready?"

"Is this barbecued beef sandwich hot?" Joel asked. "I like hot stuff."

"I don't know if you should order it," Ben advised, getting an idea. "It's too hot to handle."

"Nothing's too hot for me," Joel said, handing Ben his menu. "That's what I'll have."

"If you say so," Ben murmured, writing it down on his pad.

"One other thing," Joel said.

"Yes?"

"Do I know you?"

*This is it,* Ben's mind screamed. *It's all over. I'm going to be exposed.*

Ben swallowed over the lump of fear in his throat. "Know *me*?"

Joel nodded his head and squinted at Ben. "You look familiar. I have a funny feeling we've met before, but I can't remember where."

"You're probably confusing me with someone else," Ben said, trying not to sound nervous. Any second now he expected Joel to jump to his feet and point a finger at him, shouting, *Who do you think you're fooling, Ben? I know it's you!*

"I don't think so," Joel insisted. "I never forget a face."

Suddenly Ben had an idea. And not a very nice one. "I know!" he exclaimed. "I'll bet you're confusing me with my identical twin sister, Jenny. She works as a waitress out by the pool. I'll bet you met her. She's going to *die* when I tell her you were asking about her."

"You have a twin sister?" Joel asked.

Ben nodded. "Do you have a girlfriend? I know Jenny would *love* to go out with you! Do you want me to ask her for you? I can go out to the pool."

"No!" Joel shouted, jumping to his feet. "I don't want to go out with your sister. Actually, I'm seeing someone."

"Too bad," Ben murmured. "Jenny will be so disappointed."

After taking everyone else's order, Ben went out to the kitchen. When his orders were ready, he loaded up his tray.

Except for Joel's sandwich.

If hot was what he wanted, hot was what he was going to get.

Ben opened the sandwich and added a few extra ingredients. First came the red-hot peppers, followed by sliced jalapeños and a smear of hot Chinese mustard. To top it all off, he found a bottle of Tabasco sauce and poured it all over the sandwich before putting the top back on.

Out in the dining room, Ben served everyone their lunch. He saved Joel for last, placing his sandwich in front of him.

"Enjoy," he said.

"Don't worry," Joel stated. "I will."

*I wouldn't be too sure of that,* Ben thought smugly. He walked a short distance away and watched as Joel tackled his sandwich. He picked it up and took a huge bite. Ben watched Joel's face. At first he chewed normally. But then, as he continued to chew, his face turned bright red. His eyes started bulging out. Tears began streaming down his cheeks.

Joel jumped out of his chair, clutching his throat.

"Water!" he gasped. "Water!"

He reached for his water glass on the table, but it was empty. As were all the other glasses on the table. Ben had made sure he hadn't refilled them and he'd "forgotten" to bring out the sodas they'd ordered.

"Water!" Joel cried, looking around frantically. "Water!"

"Right away!" Ben cried, grabbing the water pitcher from the stand behind him. He hurried toward Joel, who snatched the pitcher out of his hands and started drinking out of it. Water dribbled down the front of his shirt and shorts as he chugged from the pitcher.

Out of the corner of his eye, Ben could see Lexie standing in the entrance to the dining room, looking around. She was probably searching for him. When her eyes fell upon Joel, she started laughing hysterically. Ben couldn't blame her. It was a funny sight. The front of Joel's clothes were all wet and his face was flaming red. He was a mess.

Lexie's laughter had an effect on the rest of the dining room. Soon other diners began laughing at Joel, who didn't like it. He shoved the empty water pitcher at Ben and stormed out of the dining room.

Ben returned to Joel's table, removing his sandwich. "Guess he was wrong," he commented to Joel's friends. "It was too hot for him to handle."

# Chapter 15

"Mission accomplished!" Ben announced triumphantly upon his return to his bungalow.

Ray tossed down the magazine he'd been skimming through while waiting for Ben to come back. "Did anyone recognize you?"

Ben pulled off the curly red wig, running his fingers through his hair. He grabbed a tissue from the box on the dresser and started wiping off his makeup. "I had a close call with Joel. He sat at one of my tables."

"Was he suspicious?"

"He was too busy making nasty jokes with his pals to notice it was me," Ben called out from the bathroom while washing his face. "But I fixed him."

"How?"

Ben emerged from the bathroom, drying

his face with a towel. He told Ray the entire story, and by the time he was finished, Ray was holding his sides, laughing. "I wish I could have been there to see it."

Ben chuckled. "He'll never eat a barbecue sandwich again."

"Did Lexie stick around?"

Ben took off his waitress uniform and changed back into his shorts and T-shirt. "She was gone when I came back out of the kitchen."

"Guess she saw you weren't there and went looking for you."

"She was late," Ben said. "I wonder what kept her."

Suddenly there was a knock on the door, followed by Lexie's voice. "Ben? Are you in there?"

"Quick!" Ben ordered, tossing the wig and waitress uniform at Ray. "Hide!"

Ray ducked into the nearest bedroom as Ben hurried to the door. "I'm coming." He held the door wide open for Lexie and smiled at her. "Hi."

"I'm sorry I stood you up for lunch, but my parents didn't call when they were supposed to," Lexie said, walking into the bungalow. "They finally called when I was on my way out the door to meet you. I don't blame you for not waiting."

"That's okay. I was late, too. I fell asleep on the beach."

"I hope you didn't burn."

"I'm fine. What's new with your parents?"

"They're having a blast. All they do is sit on the beach and sip tropical drinks. But wait'll you hear my news!"

Ben had never seen Lexie so excited. Her cheeks were flushed and her eyes were sparkling. "What is it?"

"I'm going away!"

"Going away? Where?"

"To Hawaii for two weeks! It's an early birthday present from my parents."

Two weeks without Lexie. Ben didn't know how he'd be able to stand it. "I'll miss you."

"Don't worry. I'll be back."

Ben had hoped Lexie would say she was going to miss him, but she hadn't. All she could think about was her trip.

"When are you leaving?"

"Tonight."

Lexie was so happy. He couldn't spoil her trip. He couldn't tell her how he'd been deceiving her. He'd wait until she came back and then he'd tell her the truth.

"I didn't tell you all my news," Lexie added. "My parents said I could have a clambake for my seventeenth birthday."

"When's your birthday?"

"The day I come back."

"Then I'll have to spend the time you're away finding the perfect present," Ben said.

"All I want is for you to be at my party," Lexie said. "Promise me you'll be there."

Ben crossed his heart. "I'll be there. Promise."

"I better go. I've got a million things to do before my flight. I'll see you when I get back, okay?"

"Okay."

With those final words, Lexie raced out of the bungalow. It was only after she was gone that Ben realized she had left without kissing him good-bye.

"I've never seen you so down in the dumps," Ray complained to Ben a week later.

"I miss Lexie," Ben said. "I can't wait till she gets home next week."

"Can't you look on the bright side?" Ray asked.

"What bright side?"

"You wouldn't have been able to see her

anyway. Your parents grounded you for two weeks. Lexie's trip to Hawaii solved your problem and you didn't even have to lie to her."

"I would have figured out *some* way to see her before going home," Ben said.

"Well, you better get used to not seeing her."

"What are you talking about?"

"What's going to happen once classes start in September?" Ray asked. "You're going to be stuck here in Berkley Heights and she's going to be at her fancy private school in Southvale."

"Don't remind me."

"Ben, the summer's not going to last forever," Ray reminded him. "If Lexie really means a lot to you, you're going to have to tell her the truth. Time's running out. It's already the end of July."

"I know. I know," Ben admitted. "But I don't want to think about that today, okay? I have to buy Lexie a birthday present."

"What did you want to get?"

"Something special."

Ray rolled his eyes. "What does *that* mean? Is it animal, vegetable, or mineral?"

"It has to be something that no one else would think of getting her," Ben said.

"To show her that you know her the way no one else does." Ray nodded his head. "Good strategy. I'll have to try that out on Ashley."

"It's not strategy," Ben snapped. "I want to find Lexie the perfect gift. Something she'll really love."

"How much did you want to spend?"

"Money doesn't matter."

Ray's eyes bugged out of his head. "It doesn't? I'll have to remind you of those words when *my* birthday rolls around. Did I mention I've had my eye on a portable CD player?"

Ben smacked Ray on the top of his head. "Will you get serious?"

"Fine," Ray stated, rubbing his head. "By my calculations, you've made *zero* this summer. Don't tell me you're going to dip into your savings account again."

"If I have to, I will. But I got paid today and I also made some nice tips this week."

"Ben, I know you want to get Lexie a nice gift, but don't go overboard. If she dumps you, not only are you not going to have a girlfriend, but you're also going to be flat broke."

"I'm not going to go overboard," Ben insisted. "Expensive things don't matter to

Lexie. I have to find a gift that shows her my feelings. It has to say something."

"What do you want it to say?"

" 'I love you,' " Ben said. "It has to say 'I love you' so every time Lexie looks at it, she knows how much she means to me."

"Why is that so important?" Ray asked.

"Because after I tell her the truth, she may never want to talk to me again," Ben whispered. "She might not give me a chance to explain and I don't want her to believe that everything I told her was a lie. It wasn't. Except for pretending to be someone I wasn't, I didn't ever lie to Lexie about my feelings, and I want her to know that."

"Have you told Lexie you love her?"

Ben shook his head.

"Why not?" Ray asked.

"What if she doesn't feel the same way?"

"You won't know unless you tell her," Ray said. "And you know something else?"

"What?"

"She just might surprise you. She might say 'I love you' back. How do you know Lexie is having a great time in Hawaii? She could be missing you just as much as you're missing her."

Ray's words lifted Ben's spirits. Could Ray be right? Could Lexie be missing him?

Could she have fallen in love with him and realized it only after she went away? It was almost too much to hope for.

He'd only know for sure when Lexie got back.

# Chapter 16

"Miss me much?" Lexie asked.

Before Ben could answer, Lexie ran out of her bungalow and threw her arms around him in a hug.

Ben wrapped his arms around Lexie and hugged her back. It felt good to hold her in his arms again. He'd missed her so much.

"Hey," Lexie said, laughing, "you're practically crushing me. You must have really missed me."

Ben loosened his hold on Lexie and took a step back. "I did," he admitted. "A lot. The entire two weeks dragged by. I started to think today was never going to get here. I can't believe you're back and standing in front of me."

"Believe it."

"You look terrific."

Lexie's two weeks in Hawaii had given

her a deep, dark tan. She was wearing a brightly colored flowered sarong, a white bikini top, and a seashell necklace.

"I missed you, too," Lexie admitted. "I thought of you the entire time."

"You did?"

Lexie nodded. "I would have called, but we stayed on a remote island that didn't have any telephones. They didn't even have televisions or radios. Two weeks without any music or MTV! It was barbaric!"

"I'm really glad you're back."

"Come inside," Lexie urged, pulling Ben by the arm. "I just got back from the airport and was unpacking."

Ben followed Lexie into her bungalow. Scattered throughout the room were open suitcases and shopping bags. He looked around for Astrid but didn't see her slinking around.

"Where's Astrid?" he asked.

"Still at the vet. His office closes at six and I didn't have time to pick her up. She'll be back tomorrow."

"Ready to hiss and scratch at me, I'm sure."

"That's just her way of saying she likes you," Lexie said.

"I wonder what she'd do if she hated me," Ben murmured.

"I brought back presents for everyone. Yours is on the couch."

"You didn't have to bring me back anything."

"I wanted to." Lexie sat next to Ben on the couch and placed a wrapped box in his lap. As she did, the charm bracelet on her wrist jingled. "Who says you get to buy all the presents? Now open it."

Ben tore away the wrapping paper and lifted the lid of the box. Pushing aside the mounds of tissue paper inside, he found a Hawaiian shirt covered with tropical flowers.

"I thought you could wear it to my birthday party tonight. See, it matches my sarong. We'll be a matched set."

"It's great," Ben said.

"Only one more hour till my party. I can't wait!" Lexie squealed. "It's going to be a blast!"

"Speaking of birthdays, I've got a birthday present for you. Do you want it now or later?"

"What a silly question!" Lexie exclaimed. "I want it now, now, now! There isn't anything I love more than opening presents!"

"Are you sure?" Ben asked.

Lexie pretended to think. "Well, I do like kissing you and it has been two weeks since our last kiss. Think you could spare one?"

"I thought you'd never ask," Ben answered, pressing his lips to Lexie's.

"Mmm," Lexie whispered, wrapping her arms around Ben's neck and snuggling close to him. "Just as sweet as I remembered."

Ben gave Lexie a second kiss, then hopped off the couch. "I'll be right back."

He hurried next door to Ben Holt's bungalow and retrieved Lexie's present from the dresser. It was a big box, wrapped in pink foil and topped with a white ribbon. When he returned to Lexie's bungalow with the box, her eyes widened.

"Happy birthday," Ben said, placing the box next to her on the couch. "I hope you like it."

Lexie turned the box around, examining it from all sides. "It's so big! What is it?"

"I'm not telling," Ben said. "You'll have to open it and see."

Lexie ripped away the pink foil covering the box. When she lifted the lid and gazed inside, she gasped. She tore her eyes away from the box and stared at Ben, then looked back into the box.

It was the reaction Ben had been hoping for. He'd racked his brains trying to find the perfect gift for Lexie, but what did you buy the girl who had everything? And then he remembered. Remembered what meant so much to Lexie.

"I don't believe it," she murmured.

"Do you like it?" Ben asked.

"How could I not?" Lexie whispered. "No one's ever given me anything so wonderful. I can't wait to use them."

Inside the box was an assortment of colored pencils, tubes of oil paint, watercolors, charcoal pencils, sketch pads, brushes, rolled canvases, and a black leather portfolio with a zipper.

"Since you're into art, I thought you could experiment with different kinds of materials," Ben explained. "That way you'd find out which you like best." Ben paused. "Hey, what's wrong? Why are you crying?"

"I'm not crying," Lexie sniffed.

"Sure looks like you're crying to me."

"Something got in my eye."

"If you say so."

"I say so." Lexie wiped away the tears brimming around the corners of her eyes.

"This is the best birthday present anyone's ever given me."

"Even better than a trip to Hawaii?" Ben asked dubiously.

"Even better than a trip to Hawaii," Lexie said. "No one's ever listened to me when I've talked about my art. About how much it means to me. But you listened and you gave me this wonderful gift."

Ben shrugged. "I know how badly you want to be an artist. I thought maybe I could help make your dream come true."

"I'm never going to forget this birthday as long as I live," Lexie said, wrapping her arms around Ben's chest.

"I didn't mean to make you sad, Lexie," Ben said, holding her close and whispering in her ear. "All I want to do is make you happy. That's all I've ever wanted to do. I'd never hurt you. Even if it seemed like I meant to, like I did it on purpose, I didn't."

Lexie lifted her head up, staring at Ben in confusion. "What do you mean?"

*Do it! Do it now!* the little voice in Ben's head screamed. *Tell her the truth!*

Ben had vowed to tell Lexie everything when she returned from Hawaii. To explain why he had lied to her. But the words wouldn't come out. They were stuck in his throat. Frozen.

He was afraid of her reaction.

He was afraid of losing her.

"Is there something you want to tell me?" Lexie asked.

Ben shook his head. "It's nothing important. It can wait."

He couldn't tell her the truth. Not tonight. It would spoil her birthday and he didn't want to do that. She was so happy. He'd wait until tomorrow and he'd tell her the truth then.

Lexie slipped out of Ben's embrace. "I'm going to pop into the bathroom and put on a little makeup. Then we can go down to the beach for my party."

"Okay."

"I brought back some macadamia nuts from Hawaii. They're on top of the coffee table."

Ben reached for a handful of the nuts and started munching on them while Lexie continued talking to him from inside the bathroom.

"You'll never guess who's going to be at my party tonight," she called out.

"Who?"

"My cousin Ryan. I'll bet you can't wait to see him again."

Ben choked on the macadamia nuts he was chewing. He started coughing.

Ryan.

From Bennington Academy.

And the only person at Lexie's party who would know Benjamin Harris *wasn't* Benjamin Holt.

"Are you okay?" Lexie called out.

"Fine," Ben gasped, even though he wasn't. There was no way he could go to Lexie's birthday party. If he did, he'd be exposed. And in front of all her friends. He could imagine the smug smiles on Pam's and Dionne's faces. Lexie would be humiliated. He couldn't do that to her.

Lexie emerged from the bathroom. "I'm ready to go."

Ben snatched his Hawaiian shirt off the couch. "I'm going to go next door and change. I'll meet you on the beach."

"I'll wait for you," Lexie offered, following him out the door.

"You're the birthday girl," Ben scolded. "If you wait for me, you'll be late, and you can't be late to your own birthday party."

"Well, don't take too long," Lexie warned. "I can't have any fun until you're there."

"Try to," Ben said. "Please?"

"I'll try, but it'll be hard."

"How come?"

"Because you're the only person I want to spend my birthday with," Lexie admitted. "You're the only guest who matters." She headed for the path that led to the beach and looked over her shoulder one last time. "I'll be counting the minutes until you show up."

Ben watched as Lexie disappeared from sight, wishing he could follow her, wishing he could be at her party.

But he couldn't.

And the only person he had to blame was himself.

# Chapter 17

Ben figured Lexie would be angry, but he hadn't thought she would be *this* angry. From the second he had knocked on the door of her bungalow and she had opened the door, she'd given him the deep freeze. No hello. No smile. Nothing. She had left the door open and walked back inside with Ben following after her.

He almost wished she would scream and yell at him. Throw something. Instead she sat on the couch in silence, staring at him coldly, not saying a word.

Of course, he couldn't blame her for being mad. He hadn't shown up for her party.

"I'm sorry," Ben said, trying to break the awkward silence.

"You're *sorry*? Is that all you can say?" Lexie demanded, her voice dripping with ice. "I spent the entire night wondering where you were."

"I know," Ben whispered. He'd watched the party from a distance, hiding out of sight behind an outcrop of rocks on the beach. While everyone else was laughing and dancing, he could see Lexie hadn't been having a good time. On more than one occasion she'd left the party. He hadn't followed her but knew she'd gone to Ben Holt's bungalow to search for him.

It hurt knowing he'd spoiled Lexie's birthday.

"Where were you?" she asked.

Last night, after seeing how he'd made Lexie unhappy, Ben had vowed to tell her the truth. All of it. But now he couldn't do it. The timing wasn't right. She was *so* angry. If he told her the truth, she wouldn't listen to any of his reasons for why he'd lied to her. She'd only get angrier.

"I had an emergency," Ben said, hoping Lexie didn't ask for details. He didn't want to have to make up another story. He'd told so many lies, he was starting to lose track!

"You couldn't even leave me a note?" Lexie asked.

Hearing the hurt tone in her voice, Ben

felt worse. He started to answer, but Lexie held up a hand.

"Save it," she snapped. "I don't want to hear your excuses. In fact, I don't ever want to listen to anything you have to say again."

"But Lexie . . ."

"You let me down, Ben," Lexie whispered. She clutched a throw pillow against her chest. She was trying hard not to cry, but her lower lip trembled and her eyes were moist. She blinked her eyes, holding back the tears. "You were the one person I thought I could count on. Who I thought wouldn't let me down. I wanted to spend my birthday with someone special. I wanted to spend it with *you*. But I didn't. I spent it all by myself."

"You can count on me, Lexie," Ben insisted. "You can trust me."

Lexie brushed the back of a hand across her eyes. "How can I, after what you did last night?"

"It'll never happen again. I promise."

"You promised to come to my party," Lexie threw back. "But you didn't, did you?"

"No," Ben admitted, looking down at the carpet. "I didn't."

"So why should I believe you?"

"Don't I deserve a second chance?" Ben

pleaded. He lifted his head and locked eyes with Lexie. "I feel awful! I didn't mean to hurt you, Lexie. Please give me a second chance. Haven't we been a great couple so far? Don't give up on us."

Lexie stared at Ben, then she threw the pillow in her arms at him. It bounced off his chest and fell to the floor. "You don't deserve to be so cute!" she shouted. "Stop looking at me with those sad eyes."

"I can't help it."

"Don't you ever do what you did to me last night again! If you do, it's over between us, I swear it. I was worried sick! I thought something had happened to you."

"You were worried about me?"

"Yes."

"How come?"

Lexie huffed in exasperation, folding her arms across her chest. "That's a silly question."

Ben could sense Lexie's anger was melting. She was still mad, but not as mad as she'd been a while earlier. "No, it isn't," he insisted. "Tell my why."

"Because I care about you."

"You do?"

Lexie nodded her head. "Yes, I do."

*Do you love me?* Ben wanted to ask but

didn't. He didn't have the courage to say the words out loud. What if Lexie gave him an answer he didn't want to hear? What if she told him she *didn't* love him? That she could *never* love him?

He'd be devastated.

Most of all, he didn't have the courage to do what he'd been wanting to do all summer: tell Lexie he loved her.

"I'll make it up to you," he said.

"How?"

Ben reached into the back pocket of his jeans and pulled out two tickets.

"What are those?" Lexie asked.

"Tickets to the masquerade cruise on Saturday night." They'd cost him a fortune, but he wanted to do something special for Lexie. "Want to go?"

"You bet!" Lexie exclaimed, excitement filling her voice. "Everyone I know is going."

"Is your cousin Ryan going?" Ben asked, trying to sound casual. "Or did he head home after your party?"

"Ryan didn't make it to the party last night," Lexie said. "He called and left a message at the front desk, unlike *some* people I know."

Ben winced. "Ouch. That hurt."

Lexie smiled sweetly at Ben. "It was supposed to."

"How come he didn't show?"

"He sprained his ankle playing touch football yesterday afternoon. He has to stay off it for a week."

"Bummer," Ben said.

"I'm going to change into my bikini," Lexie said, getting off the couch. "Then we can go down to the beach. Unless you pull another disappearing act."

Ben made a face at Lexie. "Very funny. I'll be right here, waiting."

Lexie pointed a finger at Ben. "You better, otherwise you'll get to see what I'm like when I'm *really* mad."

While waiting for Lexie to change, Ben made a decision.

Saturday night was the night he would tell her the truth.

No more excuses.

No more putting it off.

Saturday night he would tell her everything.

He decided something else, too.

Saturday night was also the night he would tell Lexie he loved her.

# Chapter 18

"What a great costume!" Lexie raved when Ben arrived to pick her up for the masquerade cruise.

"You really think so?"

Ben hadn't rented a costume, but put one together himself: He was a rebel from the fifties. He was wearing a white T-shirt, blue jeans, a black motorcycle jacket, and biker boots. He'd slicked his hair back, rolled up the bottoms of his jeans, and put up the collar of his motorcycle jacket. He was even wearing a pair of dark sunglasses.

"Absolutely."

"You look pretty great, too," Ben said.

Lexie was dressed as a gypsy in an off-the-shoulder white blouse and long red skirt. She was wearing wide silver hoop earrings and had her hair tied back with a colorful scarf.

"Can you tell my fortune?" Ben asked.

Lexie took Ben's palm in her hand and started tracing a line with her finger. "I see lots of fun in your future."

"What kind of fun?"

Lexie peered closely at Ben's palm. "Dancing."

"Anything else?"

Lexie glanced up at Ben, a smile twitching on her lips. "Maybe some kissing."

Ben couldn't help himself. He leaned his head closer to Lexie's, whispering in her ear, "Anytime soon?"

"How about now?" Lexie said, turning her head so that her lips met Ben's.

They kissed, and when it ended, Ben caressed Lexie's cheek. "Can I tell you something?"

"Sure."

"It's something I've never told a girl before."

"Ooh, a secret. I love secrets."

Ben grinned. "It's not a secret."

"Tell me," Lexie urged. "I'm dying of suspense."

Ben took a deep breath to calm his pounding heart. His palms were sweaty and he wiped them against the sides of his jeans. It was now or never. He'd vowed to do this and he was going to. No matter what. "I love you."

Lexie blinked at Ben. Her eyes were wide with shock and she seemed stunned.

"What's wrong?" Ben asked.

"I've never had a guy tell me he loves me," Lexie admitted.

"Not even Joel?"

"Not even Joel. But if he had, I wouldn't have believed him."

"How come?"

"Come on, Ben! You've met him. He's a self-centered jerk. The only person he loves is himself."

"Do you believe me?" Ben asked. "That I love you?"

"Yes," Lexie said. "I do."

"I've been wanting to tell you all summer," Ben confessed, "but I couldn't. I was afraid."

"Afraid of what?"

"I know Joel really hurt you and you've been taking things slowly. With us, I mean. I didn't want to scare you off. Telling someone you love them is pretty intense. And there was other stuff, too."

"Like what?"

Ben shrugged. "A lot of things. I'll tell you later." He glanced at his watch. "We better hurry or we're going to miss the boat."

Lexie pressed a hand on Ben's arm. "Wait a second. I've got a secret to tell you, too."

"You do?"

Lexie nodded her head. "Can you guess what it is?"

Ben shrugged. "I haven't got a clue."

"I love you, too."

Ben couldn't believe what he was hearing. It was what he'd been dreaming of all summer. Lexie loved him!

"I started to realize it when I was in Hawaii," Lexie confessed. "I missed you so much! But then I knew for sure after you gave me my birthday present. Remember what we were talking about at the dance? Suddenly I *knew* I loved you. I was going to tell you at my birthday party, but you didn't show up. That's what made me so mad."

"You really love me?" Ben whispered. Part of him was almost afraid that this was a dream. That at any second his alarm clock would go off, taking him away from the most wonderful moment of his life.

"Didn't you hear me?" Lexie teased. "I'll say it again. Real slow. *I love you.*" Lexie slipped her hand into Ben's. "Come on. We better get going, otherwise we're going to be left behind."

They hurried down to the beach and the dock where the cruise ship was tied. Once on board, they found themselves surrounded by other costumed couples. There were mummies, genies, vampires, and ghosts. There were superheroes like Batman and Wonder Woman, and supervillains like Catwoman and the Joker.

Dionne, Pam, and Joel were also on the cruise. Ben and Lexie ran into them at the juice bar. Dionne was dressed as Cruella de Vil from *101 Dalmatians* (which Ben thought was the perfect costume for her), Pam was dressed as a mermaid, and Joel was dressed as the Riddler.

"I love your costume, Lexie," Dionne gushed.

"Me too," Pam said. "I bet you win first prize."

"Thanks," Lexie said. "But it looks like the competition for best costume is going to be stiff."

Ben kept waiting for Joel to say something, but he didn't. Instead, he ignored them, which was fine with Ben.

After leaving the juice bar, Ben and Lexie spent the rest of the evening having a wonderful time. They danced every chance they got, took walks around the deck holding hands, and enjoyed the buffet table, heaping their plates with all kinds of delicious munchies like pizza rolls and baby back ribs.

Toward the end of the night, when the DJ took a break between songs, Ben and Lexie returned to the deck to be alone. Leaning against the railing, they stared out at the water, holding hands in the moonlight.

"What are we going to do when school starts next month and you have to go back to Bennington Academy?" Lexie asked.

"We'll figure out a way to see each other."

"It won't be the same as seeing you every day," Lexie sighed. "Having you right next door. I guess it was my lucky day when Astrid climbed up that tree. If she hadn't, I'd have never met you."

Lexie's mention of the day they met suddenly made Ben feel guilty. He'd been putting it off all night, but now he had to face it. It was time to tell Lexie the truth.

"Lexie, there's something else I have to tell you."

"Can it wait?" Lexie pointed to the couples heading back inside. "They're going to announce the winner of the best costume."

"I guess," Ben reluctantly agreed. "But after the winner's announced, can we come back out here?"

"You can tell me whatever you want," Lexie promised.

Ben and Lexie followed everyone back inside. In the center of the dance floor, the DJ stood holding a microphone.

"We're heading to shore," he announced, "but until we get back, there's still lots of fun ahead. First we're going to announce the winner for best costume of the night, and then we're going to draw the winning ticket from our raffle. I hope everyone bought a ticket because the winner gets a thousand dollars!"

"Do you have your ticket stub?" Lexie asked.

Ben patted his back pocket. He'd bought a ticket when they'd boarded the boat. "Cross your fingers."

The winner of the best costume turned out to be a girl who came to the dance as a candy cane, wrapped from head to toe in layers of white and red ribbons. After she left with her prize, the DJ dipped his hand into a fishbowl filled with tickets.

"This is it. The moment you've all been waiting for. Who's going to go home with a thousand dollars?" He pulled out a ticket and stared at the name written on the back. "The winner is Benjamin Holt!"

"Ben, you won!" Lexie shrieked happily.

"I don't believe it," Ben gasped, stunned. All the money he'd spent this summer he had back, with some extra!

"Go claim your prize," Lexie said.

Ben walked to the center of the dance floor. As he headed toward the DJ, he noticed something.

Someone else was walking toward the DJ.

It was a dark-haired guy, dressed all in black with a black cowboy hat on his head.

The DJ looked confused. He turned to Ben and then the guy dressed in black.

"Which one of you is Benjamin Holt?" he asked.

"I am," Ben answered.

"I am," the guy dressed in black answered.

"What a coincidence," the DJ said. "Two guys with the same name. Well, only one of you can be a winner. You'll have to give me your ticket stubs, so I can compare them to the one I have."

As Ben handed over his ticket stub, he realized the truth.

The awful truth.

His stomach tied up in knots. Sweat began forming around his forehead.

Standing across from him was the *real* Benjamin Holt.

"What's going on?" Lexie asked, coming to Ben's side.

"I'll tell you what's going on," Joel exclaimed, joining the group with Dionne. He pointed a finger at Ben. "You've been fooled. We all have! This guy has been pretending to be someone he's not!"

"What are you talking about?" Lexie asked.

"I don't know the real name of the guy you've been dating all summer, but it's *not* Benjamin Holt."

"That's a lie," Lexie stated.

"No, it isn't," Joel said. "It's the truth." He pointed a finger at the guy dressed in black. "That's the real Benjamin Holt. I recognize his face from the Bennington Academy yearbook."

"And I recognize him from the Bennington dances I've been to," Dionne added. "I never saw your Ben at any of them. I said that the very first time I met him. Don't you remember, Lexie?"

"You're lying," Lexie whispered. "Both of

you. You'll say anything to make me break up with Ben."

"We're not the ones lying," Joel said. "We're telling you the truth. *He's* the liar. He's been lying to you all summer."

Lexie turned to Ben with a confused look on her face. "What they're saying isn't true, is it?"

It was the moment Ben had been dreading all summer. His worst nightmare come to life.

"Lexie, I can explain."

Lexie gasped, clasping a hand over her mouth. "Explain what? Who are you?"

"Lexie . . ."

"Who are you?" Lexie screamed. "If you're not the real Benjamin Holt, what were you doing in his bungalow the day we met? Why did you pretend to be someone you're not?"

"My real name is Benjamin Harris," Ben admitted. "I work at the hotel."

"You work at the hotel? Doing what?"

"I'm a maid. I clean rooms."

"He's a maid!" Joel laughed. "*A maid.* I don't believe it!"

Everyone on the dance floor and sitting at the surrounding tables stared at Ben and

Lexie. He could feel their eyes burning into his back. He could hear their whispers and see their pointed fingers.

Lexie broke free of the crowd and ran from the dance floor. Ben hurried after her, but she disappeared in the crowd. "Lexie! Wait! Let me explain."

When Ben couldn't find Lexie anywhere inside, he headed outside and started searching the decks. A half hour later he found her on the lowest deck sitting on a lounge chair, crying. He placed a hand on her shoulder, but she angrily shoved it away.

"Go away! Leave me alone!"

"But I want to explain."

Lexie looked up at Ben. Her face was streaked with tears. "You said you loved me," she cried.

"I do. With all my heart." Ben sat next to Lexie, trying to pull her hands into his, but she snatched them away. "You have to listen to me. You have to let me tell you why I pretended to be Benjamin Holt."

"It was a lie," Lexie said. "All a horrible lie. You never cared about me. You never loved me. You were playing a horrible game with me."

"No, I wasn't. Even though I pretended to

be someone I wasn't, I never lied when I told you how I felt. I love you, Lexie. I'm telling you the truth."

"The truth?" Lexie shrieked. "You don't know anything about the truth. You've been lying to me all summer. Laughing at me behind my back and making me look like a fool. You've embarrassed me in front of all my friends."

"I didn't mean to. I didn't mean to hurt you. All I wanted was to get to know you. I didn't think you'd talk to me if you knew who I really was, but I'm the same person you fell in love with."

Lexie shook her head. "No, you're not. I thought you were someone else."

"Someone rich?" Ben demanded.

"No!" Lexie shouted. "I thought you were someone I could trust! But you're a liar!" Lexie took off the charm bracelet Ben had bought for her and threw it at him. "I hate you!" she cried. "I wish I'd never met you. I wish you'd drowned when you'd fallen into that pool!"

"If you'd only listen," Ben pleaded.

Lexie jumped off the lounge chair. The ship had pulled back to shore and crew members were lowering the plank that led down to the dock. Lexie started to run toward it, but then stopped and looked back at Ben. "I don't want to listen. I don't ever want to listen to anything you have to say again. It's over between us, Ben. Over. I never want to see you again."

# Chapter 19

"What's the matter, Ben?" Dougie asked, sitting next to his brother on the front steps of their house. "Why are you so sad? Is it because school starts next week?"

Ben ran a hand over Dougie's head, messing his hair. "No, squirt. It's not that."

"Then what is it? You never smile anymore. Ever since the night you went to that costume dance."

Ben hadn't realized his little brother was so observant. "It's a lot of things. You'll understand when you get older."

Dougie made a face. "That means it has to do with girls."

"Girls aren't so bad. You'll see."

"Want one of my cookies?" Dougie asked, holding out a package. "They're Oreos. I'll even let you have two. It'll make you feel better."

"Thanks," Ben said, taking the two cookies his brother offered.

"I'll see you later," Dougie said, getting to his feet.

"Where are you going?"

"To Jack Gold's house. We're going to watch videos. Want to do something when I get back?"

"You bet."

After Dougie left, Ben took off the top of his Oreo and ate the white stuff inside. Then he popped the cookie part into his mouth and tried to figure out what to do with the rest of his day.

His job with the club had ended last Friday. Luckily, he hadn't been fired, but if he had, it wouldn't have made a difference because he'd won the thousand dollars in the cruise raffle. The reason he hadn't been fired was because of the real Ben Holt, who turned out to be a cool guy and didn't say anything to the club's management.

It had been a month since the disaster on the cruise ship. After Lexie ran off the ship, Ben had gone back inside, where he'd learned that he was the Ben Holt who'd won the raffle. After collecting his prize money, he'd felt a tap on his shoulder.

It was Benjamin Holt.

"Mind telling me what's going on?" he asked. "I feel like I walked into the middle of a movie."

Ben sighed. "It's a long story."

Ben told the real Ben Holt everything. When he had finished, Ben Holt stared at him.

"You must be crazy about this girl if you did all that."

"I am," Ben admitted, "but I shouldn't have let things go on as long as they did. It wasn't right."

"You did it all for a good reason. What's wrong with that?"

"Lexie doesn't feel that way. She hates me."

"She'll get over it."

Ben sighed. "You think so?" It was too much to hope for. "She's really mad at me."

"She needs to cool off. Give her some space and then make your move."

"I guess you're going to tell the club what I've been doing all summer," Ben said. "Impersonating you."

Ben Holt's answer stunned Ben, who had expected him to be mad.

"Why should I? It's not like you deliberately planned to be me. It sort of happened. By accident. Besides, you're already in enough hot water with your girlfriend. You don't need me adding to it."

"You're not going to say *anything*?" Ben asked.

"Just don't pretend to be me anymore," Ben Holt warned. "Deal?"

"Deal," Ben agreed, holding his hand out for a shake. "Are you going to be around for the rest of the summer?"

"My family arrived this afternoon. We're only staying for a week."

"Maybe I'll see you around," Ben said.

"At least I'll know who to call if I want extra towels," Ben Holt said with a laugh.

Talking with Ben Holt had given Ben hope. Maybe if he gave Lexie a few days to cool off, she'd be willing to listen.

Ben Holt's advice turned out to be wrong. Lexie *didn't* cool off and she refused to have anything to do with Ben. When he called her a week after the cruise, she hung up the phone. When he knocked on her bungalow door, she refused to open it. Letters he mailed to her were returned unopened. If their paths crossed at the club, she looked the other way and pretended he didn't exist.

Ben didn't know what to do except to accept the truth.

It was over between them.

Ben heard a car horn and looked up. Ray's red Honda was parked at the curb.

"I'm driving over to Southvale to see Ashley at the hotel. She gets off work at four. Want to tag along?"

"Isn't three a crowd?"

"You've been moping around your house too long. You need to get out."

Ben popped the second Oreo into his mouth. "I do have to pick up my last paycheck."

Ray swung open the passenger door of his car. "Hop in."

Ben slid into the front seat, buckling up as Ray pulled away from the curb.

"Ashley still feels bad about not telling you when the real Ben was checking in," Ray said.

"It's not her fault. She left early that day. Besides, the truth would have come out sooner or later."

"Any progress with Lexie?"

"None."

"I know you don't want to hear this, Ben, but maybe you and Lexie weren't meant to be a couple."

Ben scowled at Ray. "Thanks, Ray. Kick me when I'm down."

"Don't get mad at me! I'm on your side.

You've been trying for weeks to get Lexie to listen to you, but she won't. Obviously you don't mean as much to her as she means to you."

Ben sighed. "I guess you're right."

After arriving at the club, Ben and Ray went their separate ways, agreeing to meet at six o'clock. Ben picked up his last paycheck and then tried to decide what he should do with himself. He could go down to the beach and soak up some sun, but he didn't want to.

There was only one place he wanted to go.

Only one person he wanted to see.

Lexie.

He knew what he was going to do was crazy, but he couldn't help himself. He had to try one last time with her.

Ben walked to Lexie's bungalow. When he got there, he stood outside her door, working up his courage. As he was about to knock on the door, he heard a voice in the back.

It was Lexie.

"Astrid! Bad girl! How did you get up there?"

Ben walked around to the back of the bungalow. The scene was identical to the one when he'd met Lexie for the first time. Astrid was perched on a tree branch with Lexie staring up at her.

"Need any help?" Ben asked.

Lexie whirled around, startled. "What do you want?" Her voice was ice cold.

Ben pointed to the branch Astrid was perched on. "I thought I'd help get her down."

"Don't bother. She'll get down on her own."

"She didn't last time."

"Then she'll stay up there and learn a lesson."

"It's no problem," Ben insisted. He started climbing up the tree.

"You don't have to do this," Lexie said.

"I want to." Ben shimmied up the tree and reached the branch Astrid was clinging to. "We've been through this before, Astrid," Ben coaxed. "You know I didn't hurt you last time, so be a nice kitty and don't scratch me."

Astrid promptly hissed and struck out with her claws.

"She still doesn't like me," Ben said. "I guess she has that in common with you."

Lexie didn't answer.

"She hates me. Just like you do. I can't

blame you for feeling that way. After all, I did lie to you, but I didn't plan it."

"I'm going inside," Lexie said. "I'm leaving today and have to finish packing. If you get Astrid down, knock on the door; otherwise I'll call someone from the front desk."

Lexie turned her back on Ben and went into her bungalow. She slammed the door shut behind her.

Lexie's message was loud and clear. She wanted nothing to do with him.

"I should leave you up here," Ben complained to Astrid, reaching out for her. "In a way, it's all your fault. If you hadn't climbed up this stupid tree in the first place, I never would have had to get you down. I wouldn't have fallen into the pool and put on that robe that made Lexie think I was Ben Holt."

Ben wrapped his hands around Astrid. Like last time, she swiped with her claws and made contact, scratching the back of his hand. And like last time, Ben released Astrid and lost his balance, falling into the pool below.

As he fell, Ben screamed.

He landed in the pool with a splash as Lexie came running out of the bungalow.

"Ben!"

As Ben sank underwater, he could hear

Lexie calling out to him, her voice filled with concern. His heart soared.

She still cared about him!

The thought thrilled Ben, until he realized Lexie was too stubborn to admit her true feelings.

Unless she thought something had happened to him.

Ben decided to teach Lexie a lesson. He held his breath and remained underwater. Above, he could hear Lexie frantically calling for him.

"Ben! Ben!"

The next thing he knew, Lexie jumped into the pool, swimming toward him. She wrapped her arms around his chest and pulled him to the surface, swimming to the side of the pool.

"Ben!" she cried. "Talk to me!"

Ben pulled himself out of the water. He clutched his head, pretending to be groggy as he sat on the edge of the pool. "What happened?"

"You fell into the pool," Lexie said, sitting next to him.

"And you pulled me out?"

Lexie nodded.

"Why didn't you let me drown?"

"I might be mad at you, but not that mad."

"I wouldn't blame you. I know I really hurt you, Lexie."

"Yes, you did," Lexie said softly.

"I never meant to lie to you. The first time we met, you thought I was Ben Holt. You were in a rush and I didn't have a chance to explain."

"You could have told me the truth the next time we met," Lexie pointed out.

"I know," Ben admitted.

"So why didn't you?"

"I wanted to go out with you so badly, I didn't think I'd have a chance if you knew the truth. I was afraid."

"You could have said something at some point. You had the entire summer."

"I tried, Lexie. I honestly did. So many times I wanted to tell you the truth, but I couldn't. There was that time on the beach, right before Dionne and Pam showed up. And then there was the night in your bungalow before we went on the masquerade cruise. I always chickened out at the last minute. Don't you remember on the cruise, right before the winner for best costume was announced? I told you I wanted to tell you something."

"I remember," Lexie whispered.

"I knew what I was doing was wrong, but I didn't know how to undo it. I've been miserable without you, Lexie. Can't we start over? You're the best thing that's ever happened to me."

"I am?"

"Yes, you are," Ben reached into the pocket of his jeans and took out the charm bracelet he'd bought Lexie at the flea market. He wrapped the bracelet around her wrist. "Will you please take this back? Even if you won't give me another chance, I want you to have it. I bought it for you."

Lexie closed the bracelet's clasp. "Thanks. I missed wearing it."

"I've missed seeing you," Ben said.

Lexie played with the charms on her bracelet, not looking at Ben. "Am I supposed to believe you? You've been known to lie."

"Even though I pretended to be Ben Holt, I never lied about my feelings. I love you, Lexie, but I guess you don't believe me." Ben got to his feet and started walking away. "Not that I blame you. I really blew it, didn't I?"

"I believe you," Lexie said softly.

"You do?" Ben gasped, turning around.

"Don't sound so shocked." Lexie gazed up at Ben, smiling. "You can be very persistent."

"I am when I don't want to lose someone who means everything to me."

"You mean everything to me, too," Lexie confessed. "You're the only person who knows the real me. It's always been hard for me to trust others with my feelings, but it wasn't hard with you. You made me feel special and it was so easy falling in love with you."

"You are special," Ben said, sitting back down next to Lexie.

"You made me feel things I'd never felt before, and when I found out you weren't who you said you were, I felt betrayed," she admitted. "I felt like you had been using me. That you were playing a game with me."

"That wasn't how it was."

"I know that now. At first I didn't want to believe it, but a lot of people told me why you did what you did."

"Who?" Ben asked.

"Your friend Ray. His girlfriend Ashley. Even the real Ben Holt." Lexie moved closer to Ben. "And then there was you. No matter how hard I tried to stay mad at you, I couldn't. I always remembered the wonderful things you did for me. How you made me feel special when we were together. That was real. Even if everything else was a lie, those magic moments weren't."

"No, they weren't." Ben said.

"For weeks I've treated you horribly."

"I deserved it."

"Other guys would have given up, but you didn't."

Ben wrapped an arm around Lexie's shoulders, drawing her close. "That's because I didn't want to give up on you. On us."

"I'm glad you didn't," Lexie said, pressing her head against Ben's chest and hugging him tightly.

"Me too," Ben whispered, hugging her back, feeling like the luckiest guy in the world. "Me too."

# Epilogue

"You're standing under the mistletoe," Ben said.

Lexie stopped sipping her eggnog and glanced up. "I guess I am."

"You know what that means."

Lexie smiled at Ben and put her glass of eggnog down on a table filled with plates of Christmas cookies. "I guess I do."

Ben wrapped his arms around Lexie as she moved closer to him. Then he lowered his head to hers and kissed her the way he always kissed her — with all the feeling he had.

"Mmm. You taste good," Ben said, tracing Lexie's lower lip with a finger. "Like cinnamon."

Lexie nibbled on Ben's finger. "It's from the eggnog." She reached for her glass. "Want a sip?"

Ben peeked up at the mistletoe and looked back at Lexie, not saying anything. But before they could kiss again, a voice from behind interrupted them.

"How about letting someone else have a turn?"

Ben and Lexie turned around to find Ray with his arm around Ashley.

"You guys act like you never see each other," Ray said. "If you're not talking to each other on the phone, one of you is either driving to Berkley Heights or the other is driving to Southvale."

"Look who's talking," Ben reminded his friend, although Ray's words were true. Despite living in two different towns, he and Lexie saw each other almost every day. An hour really wasn't a long time to drive when you wanted to be with someone you loved. And next year, when they started college, Ben and Lexie planned to go to the same school.

"Are you finished?" Ray asked. "We wouldn't want to rush you."

"It's all yours," Ben said, taking Lexie by the hand and leading her through the crowded Berkley Heights High auditorium. Practically the entire school had showed up for the annual Christmas dance.

"Where are we going?" Lexie asked.

"Where we can be alone," Ben answered as the band started playing "Jingle Bell Rock."

They left the auditorium and Ben led Lexie down a deserted hallway lined with lockers. When they came to the end of the lockers, Ben stopped.

"I guess you're wondering why I wanted us to be alone," he said.

"The thought had crossed my mind," Lexie admitted.

Ben unlocked the locker they were standing in front of and reached inside it, taking out a small gift-wrapped box. "My locker," Ben stated. He handed the box to Lexie. "This is for you. An early Christmas present."

"But I don't have anything for you," Lexie said.

"That's okay."

Lexie accepted the tiny box from Ben, shaking it against her ear.

"Open it up," Ben urged.

Lexie promptly did as he requested.

"Like it?" Ben asked.

"I love it," Lexie gasped. "How do you do it?"

"Do what?"

"How do you always find the perfect gift?"

Inside the box, nestled against cotton padding, was a charm for Lexie's charm bracelet. It was a tiny cat.

"If it wasn't for Astrid, we never would have met," Ben explained. He took the charm out of the box and attached it to one of the hooks on Lexie's charm bracelet. "And we never would have gotten back together."

"I love it," Lexie said again. She looked up from the bracelet. "And I love you." She threw her arms around Ben. "Merry Christmas, Ben."

"Merry Christmas, Lexie," Ben whispered, giving her a kiss. "Merry Christmas."

# About the Author

John Hall lives with his family in New York. When he isn't busy writing, he enjoys reading, going to flea markets, watching old movies on cable, and seeing new movies on the big screen. His previous young adult novels include the thrillers *Homecoming Queen*, *Dear Sister*, and *The Cheerleaders*. John loves to hear from his readers and you may write to him c/o Scholastic Books.